The Final Chapter

After working in London for many years, Jérôme Loubry moved to the South of France, where he still lives and works.

Born in 1976, he grew up in a village famous for its book printing business, and his aunt, who worked there, made sure he grew up surrounded by books.

JÉRÔME LOUBRY

The Final Chapter

HODDER

First published in the French language as *Le douzième chapitre*
by Editions Calmann-Lévy in 2018

First published in Great Britain in 2021 by Hodder & Stoughton
An Hachette UK company

I

Copyright © Editions Calmann-Lévy 2018
English translation © Maren Baudet-Lackner 2021

The right of Jérôme Loubry to be identified as the
Author of the Work has been asserted by him in accordance
with the Copyright, Designs and Patents Act 1988.

Maren Baudet-Lackner asserts her moral right
to be identified as the Translator of the Work.

A CIP catalogue record for this title is available from the British Library

Paperback ISBN 9781529350548
eBook ISBN 9781529350555

Typeset in Plantin Light by
Palimpsest Book Production Limited, Falkirk, Stirlingshire

Printed and bound in Great Britain by Clays Ltd, Elcograf S.p.A.

Hodder & Stoughton policy is to use papers that are natural, renewable
and recyclable products and made from wood grown in sustainable forests.
The logging and manufacturing processes are expected to conform
to the environmental regulations of the country of origin.

Hodder & Stoughton Ltd
Carmelite House
50 Victoria Embankment
London EC4Y 0DZ

www.hodder.co.uk

For Loan

*"If you're reading these pages,
then I kept my promise."*

David Malet

February 1986

Paul Vermont listened attentively as his accountant shared his calculations.

Though he knew what they would say, he never could have imagined it would all happen so fast. In only five months, his factory had lost more than thirty per cent of its customers. The information the accountant shared was hardly reassuring. The metal industry crisis had hit the region hard. No one had seen the surge in supply from Eastern Europe coming. The order book was nearly empty, and his attempts to quietly sell the factory had yet to attract any interest.

"How long?" asked the director, his face pale.

"Six months, maybe eight. There are even more obstacles now. The banks won't be able to keep helping us for much longer."

Paul stood up without a word and walked over to the crackling fireplace. He was only thirty-six, but he looked at least twenty years older at that moment. He had inherited the company from his father ten years earlier. At the time, business had been booming, and on his deathbed, the old man had thought he was providing a bright future for both his son and his employees, almost all of whom he knew by name. If he'd only known . . .

Six months. The sentence seemed unfair. Paul had put so much effort into the factory. Since the beginning of the crisis, he had always managed to keep the company afloat and had made important sacrifices: money, time, his family. He had spent so many sleepless nights refusing to accept the inevitable, hoping against hope for new contracts . . . But now, the cruel reality was before him. The figures had spoken.

Six months.

"There's no other way?"

"I'm sorry, but bankruptcy is the best solution. You'll need to explain things to your staff as soon as possible, so they can make plans for the future."

"Two hundred and eighteen people out of work . . ."

"It's not your fault, it's the economic climate," offered the accountant.

"Right, the economic climate . . ."

The bureaucrat stood up, gathered his documents, and put them away in his briefcase. He only broke the silence to mumble hesitantly, "See you in two weeks?" which sounded more like a plea than a question. He knew that Paul Vermont was made of strong stuff, but given the news he'd just received, even the most resilient of men was likely to throw in the towel. And maybe do something stupid.

"Yes," replied Paul, eventually looking away from the flames. "I'll see you in two weeks."

"Good. Don't stay cooped up in this office, Paul. Get some fresh air. It's never healthy to lock yourself up alone with your worries."

As he stepped through the door, the Vermont Steelworks accountant heard a final number.

"Seven months," Paul said gravely.

"I'm sorry?"

"We'll close in seven months. Don't tell anyone for now. I want my employees to enjoy their final summer at our holiday village. They and their families have some dark days ahead, so we'll let them bask in the sun one last time. Actually, make that eight months. That takes us through to September."

"Very well, sir."

Paul Vermont remained silent for a moment. He was unable to think clearly, he felt groggy, like a boxer after receiving an unexpected uppercut. His mind was floating aimlessly, with no lifeline in sight. He closed his eyes for a second and briefly lost his balance. He placed his hand on the mantelpiece to steady himself.

"One last summer," he whispered.

Let them stroll on the warm tarmac of Avenue des Mouettes. Let the children laugh in the waves.

Let the adults talk into the night, beer in hand, watching the sun set over the ocean.

Suddenly, in his mind's eye, he saw a woman hanging from a beam. A feeling of loneliness washed over him. He glanced furtively at the framed picture on his desk. Nine years already.

Then Paul pulled himself together. He pushed away the image of the body dangling in the air for all eternity, grabbed his keys and left. He made his way down the metal stairs to the workshop. He could already imagine the imploring looks from his employees when he told them the news. Shock, fear, anger. Losing your job in a rural region like the Limousin often meant years of unemployment. And most of the staff didn't even have degrees. Finding a decent job would be difficult, and many of them never would.

Opening the workshop door, Paul was welcomed by the familiar sounds of the factory: creaking machines, the clang of metal on metal, and crackling welding sparks. He crossed the huge room and walked down the corridor. He ran into several employees who greeted him respectfully. He wondered how many of them would spit in his face in a few months' time. How many would demand explanations he wouldn't have to give? The economic climate? Just a shield to hide behind. No one would believe it. Even he had a hard time accepting the empty excuse. Vermont Steelworks was a family company. All of the family trees in the region had at least one branch that worked in it. Everyone had a family member or two on staff. In every street, at least one person could be seen leaving early in the morning wearing grey coveralls and a security badge.

A fleeting ray of sunshine streamed through the factory

windows, bathing the steel beams, dusty, oil-stained floor, and memories of the good old days in golden light. Paul closed his eyes and let the warmth flood his face. The coming months would be painful. He had tried to sell the company without going through official channels to prevent the unfortunate reality reaching the ears of his employees, but he knew it wouldn't be long before bankruptcy became the topic on everyone's lips.

"Hello, Mr Vermont. You all right?"

When he opened his eyes, Paul found himself standing across from Franck, one of his employees, whom the others had nicknamed "Red" because of his hair. He was a stocky man whose sharp features and penetrating gaze rarely went unnoticed. But the thing most people remembered after meeting him for the first time was the long scar across his right cheek.

"Yes, Franck. I'm fine, thanks. I just needed a little air."

Paul watched as his employee went on his way. Red had joined the company two years before Paul took over from his father. A bond had formed between them the very first time they spoke. A discreet friendship based on mutual respect, a friendship neither of the men could have explained.

Often, at the end of the day, after the cooling machines had let out a final rattle, which echoed throughout the building, and the factory went quiet, the two men would meet in the director's office for a drink.

They always talked about work first, but then they would visit more personal topics, confiding in one another.

During these intimate moments, Paul occasionally spoke of Eléonore. The few times he did, Franck offered the same advice he whispered to himself every morning when he got up and every night before bed, as he tried to combat his own melancholy: "It's never a good idea to bring ghosts back to life, Mr Vermont."

*

No, it's never a good idea.
  And yet, that's what happened.
  In the summer of 1986.
  The last summer for the factory.
  The last summer of my childhood.

PART ONE

Whispers from the deep

"I have to kill you. You understand, don't you?"

"Yes," replied the girl.

"Are you scared?"

"No. Will I become a ghost?" she asked, as a sudden spark of light appeared in her eyes.

"Yes. And you'll whisper in the ears of the living for many long years. Come now. It's time."

I

Monday, 14th August 2017

"You're so lucky to be a writer! Your days must be so exciting!"

That's what I read.

That's what I hear.

And that's what I sometimes see in the incredulous, envious eyes of people who have just learned what I do for a living.

And every time, I bite my tongue to keep from saying, "If you only knew, there's nothing more boring and repetitive."

No, a writer's days are only exciting in the imaginations of those who fantasize about them. Writers are bored out of their minds. That's why they make up stories. The drab, soporific routine is in fact a necessity for the profession. For a writer, "exciting" days are the leading cause of blank pages. For publishers, they are synonymous with missed deadlines and late manuscripts.

I tried to explain that to my wife for many years.

She would retort that Hemingway fought in wars, went fishing in Cuba, and got drunk in Paris. And that he still found time to write. By way of a response, I would cite a seemingly endless list of illustrious authors who cloistered themselves in monastic solitude to write their masterpieces.

But then I gave up. Much like she abandoned the idea of me ever coming to parties or going shopping with her.

That's just the way it is.

Our personal routines have shaped our routine as a married couple. Not enough to tear us apart, but just enough to keep us distant, without either one of us putting up a fuss.

Occasionally, one of us emerges from his or her bubble to get closer to the other, restoring our relationship to its former glory. I'll find myself sitting next to her at the cinema, holding her hand as we walk down the beach, or eating across from her at one of the ridiculously expensive restaurants she loves. Or sometimes it's Sarah who slips into my world for a short while. I'll discover her sitting in the room upstairs where I write most of my novels and proofread my galleys. She'll be there, as quiet and respectful as a widow sitting vigil for her dearly departed husband.

But, while routine is necessary, beneficial, and comforting, it does have a major drawback: its precariousness.

A single grain of sand is enough to knock things out of kilter.

And that's exactly what happened on that Monday, 14th August 2017.

The calm sea of my routine suddenly grew rough and stormy. Except that . . .

Except that it wasn't just my daily routine that would be destroyed by the grain of sand. But my week. My sleep. My French windows . . .

Oh, and my past.

And yet, everything had begun as usual: Sarah had set her alarm for seven o'clock as she did every morning, even at the weekend.

She was as regular and unchanging as the waves.

I got up with her, poured her a cup of tea—*straight from the Tibetan plateau* according to the box—while she took her shower, then watched as she got ready for her day at a *normal* job. According to my wife, a *normal* job is one where you have to travel to a certain place on a daily basis to complete certain tasks and receive payment in return. She was an estate agent in the neighbouring town.

"You don't really have a job. You sit there staring at the ocean, trying to find a story worth telling. And once you find it, it'll keep you holed up in the house for months. You make money off your physical and social stagnation. And no, typing still hasn't been recognized as an Olympic sport."

I had tried to dissuade her. To reason with her. To explain that with the money my books made, she and I could go hundreds of years without working.

All to no avail.

So, every day, I watched from the corner of my eye as she put on her make-up and skirt suit. Her need to cling to a social life seemed futile and entirely uninteresting to me. It was like donning a costume for a fancy-dress party that had just been cancelled. But it was her choice.

I walked her out to the courtyard, gazing at her long legs as she folded them into her luxury coupé; a practised manoeuvre which only emphasized their beauty. I stood and watched as the car disappeared behind the gate, which hadn't closed properly for the past week. An electrical problem, no doubt.

When I stepped back inside, the fruity scent of her presence wafted through the air for several long minutes before disappearing.

Around nine o'clock, I went online to try to keep abreast of the tragedies unfolding in the outside world. I took advantage of being at my desk to check on the sales of my various books and glance at my emails. Then I poured myself a cup of coffee and sat down on the patio overlooking the sea. As I lit a cigarette, I watched the beach and waited for the old woman to walk past with her dog.

For several weeks now, she too had had a routine.

She chose the same route every day. Come rain or wind, she still took the same sandy path.

Every day, I watched her. She walked along the beach, throwing a stick for her golden retriever, who would frolic and shake itself in the waves. Then they would disappear behind the rugged stone wall at the edge of my property. I paid tribute to her ritual in my own way. I watched her pass by, staying silent, abstaining from any brusque movements. Though I was too far away to make out her features, I was certain she was beautiful, her face lined with the wrinkles of a life full of trials and victories. Every morning, I told myself it would be nice to strike up a conversation. After all, sharing the same space so often conveyed a certain intimacy on our relationship, even if she appeared oblivious to it, since I couldn't remember her ever waving in my direction.

That Monday, as I poured my second cup of coffee (just before the old woman was due to walk past), the landline rang. At that moment, the sound was just a detail and not the least bit worrying (how could I have known?). It only served to remind me that I really should make sure I always connect the answerphone as soon as I get out of bed.

I reluctantly picked up, staring at the horizon.

"Is it you?" I heard my publisher's voice ask without so much as a hello.

In addition to making lots of money from my work, Samuel was also a childhood friend. We had known each other since nursery school and had experienced all of life's milestones— both painful and joyous—together. He was the archetypal bureaucrat nearing fifty who had forgotten to take care of himself in his forties: a bit pudgy around the middle, thinning hair, and breath that reeked of the cigars he chain-smoked. However, he had the charisma of a door-to-door salesman and his business acumen had made me so rich that I was willing to overlook the rest. All that mattered to me was that he had a gift for selling my books. That and our shared memories, of course.

Usually, he only called me to ask me how my new bestseller was coming along or to let me know I had a book signing coming up (including one in Paris the following week). But that morning, his voice was tense, almost aggressive.

"Yes, it's me. Did you want to talk to Sarah?" I asked sarcastically. I knew he wasn't a big fan of my wife.

"Christ, I'm not asking if it's you on the phone, I'm asking if it was you!"

The conversation had taken a strange turn. I didn't know whether to laugh or take the same anxious, aggressive tone. I was afraid Samuel might be drinking. Because, yes, he was also very into whisky. Come to think of it, he was more than an archetype—he was a full-blown caricature.

"Was it me who what?" I asked as I opened the French windows to the patio.

A warm breeze brushed against my face.

"You haven't received one?"

"Received what?"

"Nothing at all?" Samuel insisted.

"Could we use normal sentences, maybe? It might be a bit more constructive, don't you think? This is like something out of Beckett!" I said, exasperated.

I heard Samuel give a heavy sigh and then there was silence. The sigh alerted me more than anything else. After a few seconds, he spoke again; he was calm now, but still clearly troubled.

"Have you checked your letterbox?" he asked.

"Uh, no, not yet. What's going on, Samuel?"

Silence again. But no sigh this time. It was like he was holding his breath. The way you do before announcing bad news.

"I received a brown manilla envelope this morning. It was left in my letterbox and was clearly hand-delivered. I thought it was you, who—"

"No, I didn't send you anything."

"I don't know whether I should feel relieved or more worried," he mumbled.

"You're freaking me out now. What's in the envelope?"

"It's a novel. Well, several chapters of one."

"And?"

"I don't know how to explain it. You must have received a copy. Go and check and call me back. I hope you don't find anything and that this is all just a stupid prank."

I hung up and left the patio and the beach, the waves, and the safety of my daily routine behind me as I went to confront the grain of sand that had just lodged itself in my life. I walked through the lounge, cursing Samuel aloud. "Bloody hell, if this is a joke . . . Can't he just use normal sentences like everyone else? I should ask for damages for the lost creative time . . ."

I decided to open the heavy wooden door and make my way across the tropical garden to reach the letterbox located at the entrance to our villa. But before I could do so, my feet encountered an object that would undoubtedly have sent me stumbling down the marble porch steps if it had been any heavier.

But it was just a manilla envelope.

Despite the warm breeze and the protective rhythmic sound of the waves behind me, a chilling electrical sensation pulsed through me, giving me goosebumps.

Though I didn't know it yet, by bending down to retrieve that seemingly innocent envelope, I was grabbing hold of my most precious misfortunes.

You're in for a strange surprise!

After all these years . . .

Three of you will receive this tale. Three characters who are all guilty, though each in his own way.

The first did not hear Love's song: he is the deaf man.

The second saw but was too scared to speak: he is the silent man.

And the third gave up when the solution was right before his eyes: he is the blind man.

As you read these chapters from your life, you'll probably think it's all just a bad joke.

But as you continue, you'll realize that there are too many truths buried in these lines for them to be fiction.

Each of you will receive a text without knowing the identity of the two other recipients. I won't do your work for you—you'll have to figure out who the other guilty parties are on your own.

Maybe you'll try to locate the sender, but your efforts will be in vain.

So, get comfortable.

It will be painful at times, but I hope in the end it will have been constructive.

Let me take you back in time, back to that sad summer of 1986.

And you, the deaf man, will lead us there.

2

Monday, 21st August

Seven days after finding the envelope

I can imagine you sitting in your armchair looking out at the sea. It's your favourite place, I know. You like to read there. Sometimes you write, but mostly you just study the horizon, lost in the contemplation of your success.

I suspect your analytical gaze often studies the coffee cup in front of you. You examine the porcelain, looking for a stray drop that would make the entire cup undrinkable. Your strange obsession.

Don't try to understand how I know all these intimate details. You've written so many books that anyone who wants to need only read between the lines and guess at the rest.

But the real question is this: what really happened in the summer of 1986?

So, are you ready to hear the voices from the past narrate the real story? Are you ready to listen, deaf man?

If you are, let me be the writer, let me slip into your shoes and use your "character".

*

Let me slip into your shoes and use your "character".

I was trying yet again to make sense of those final words when I heard Sarah coming down the stairs. Her heels clicked violently against the wooden steps. I wondered if the Louboutins, newly purchased in Paris, would hold up to my wife's fury or if the heels might break off before she reached the bottom.

"I'm leaving," she said simply at the foot of the stairs.

She was dignified and elegant. As always.

Even when faced with tragedy.

Her Prada sheath dress—the one I bought her during a trip to Rome—hugged her curves like a second skin. Her silky brown hair was pulled back into a ponytail and formed a halo above her angular features.

But she was cruel, too. Especially when faced with tragedy.

Forcing this image of perfection on me was not the most discreet way to show me everything I'd be missing out on until her anger faded. Until she and her suitcase decided to come back and accept my apologies.

"Sarah, wait, we can talk and—" I tried to protest.

She cocked her head to one side and raised her eyebrows. "Talk?"

"Yes, there's no point leaving. Let's discuss this," I implored.

"I've been trying to talk to you for a week, or at least to get you to listen. And for a week all my attempts have fallen on deaf ears."

"You're right, but I—"

"You won't stop, and we both know it. You're the famous writer, but you'll keep trying to decipher these pages as if they were a sacred palimpsest, and you'll forget all about the reality around you in the process. Jesus, David, don't you understand that it's just a bad joke? Look at yourself! You get out of bed every night, you barely sleep, and in the morning, you look more dead than alive!"

I stood up, leaving my armchair, but she stopped me with a sweeping wave of her hand.

"No, don't bother. Stay there watching the sea, looking for ghosts. I'll come back when you've found them. Just try not to drown."

Then she pulled out the telescopic handle on her suitcase and walked through the door without another word. A few seconds later, I heard the powerful engine of her coupé roar angrily to life and retreat from the house. It quickly became a distant murmur, barely perceptible.

She's gone.

I stood there for a while, my arms at my sides, staring at the solid wood door. The waves breaking beneath me and the echo of her final words filled the otherwise silent house.

She'll be back.

This was just like every other time our marriage had been through a storm. I didn't know what she did when she holed up at her parents' house. The important thing was that she always came back. She was smart enough to prefer retreat to confrontation. Though it was painful to watch her go, I knew that it was the best way for us to love one another without tearing each other to pieces. Usually, she came back after about a week. I would make sure to have an apology ready.

A bad joke.

That's what I had thought when I first opened the envelope. A bad joke.

Then, I continued to hope that that was all it was.

I read so many truths that I hoped with all my heart that it was just a prank, maybe a reader who wanted to pull one over on his or her favourite (or most hated) author.

But the facts in the text were much too serious and painful for it to be a joke.

So, I had to read it, again and again.

To try to understand, to unearth the truth.

For a week, I did nothing but that. And I was so absorbed in it that I forgot about Sarah . . .

Last Monday, after reading the first pages, I called Samuel. And this time, my voice was the one that sounded nervous and slightly unfamiliar.

"What the hell is this?" I asked.

"I . . . haven't . . . the foggiest!" replied my publisher.

"Have you been drinking?"

"Yes, and you should too," he advised.

"Three people?"

"I have no idea who the third is, and I have no bloody idea who is messing with us! How much have you read?"

"Just the first two chapters. I don't know if I want to keep going," I said.

"You will, even if it disgusts you. I'm on the sixth, now. I've just stopped and I'm going to drink until all the letters blur together."

"Are our copies identical?"

"No idea. Read a few sentences from the first chapter."

I read five sentences at random. Each time, Samuel assured me he had the same thing. So, our versions were twins. And I seemed to be the main character.

"There must be a reason for all this," I mumbled, like a child thinking out loud.

"There'd better be one, because if I get my hands on the bastard who sent us this text, believe me, he'll regret it! Read it or get rid of it. Personally, I'm going with the second option. I'm going to pretend like nothing happened."

"But Samuel, it *did* happen. We were young, we pushed it to the back of our minds, but this story is real."

"You're a pain in the arse! Don't forget your book signing on Saturday."

I hadn't heard from him since that phone call.

Knowing my friend as well as I did, I wasn't surprised. He could disappear for two weeks, then turn up at my door with croissants. "I needed a break!" was the concise excuse he would offer, despite his usual talkativeness.

I stepped onto the patio and looked out at the ocean.

Our house had a panoramic view of the beach. If you stood on the patio at high tide, it almost felt like you were walking on the water. When the estate agent had brought us to visit, I had just received the advance for my first book. It was a big investment, but if I published just one book a year, it would be affordable. And that's what happened. Then my two first books were turned into films, and after that into two eponymous series. We paid off the mortgage quickly. Two hundred and fifty square metres of metal and glass. Three bathrooms, six bedrooms, a jacuzzi, and several lounges, each one as big as a studio. Exotic wood, marble, and no neighbours except for the waves, the maritime pines, and the dunes and their grasses. "A real writer's house!" the agent had said in his closing argument. And now here I was, alone in this huge "writer's house" staring at the horizon wondering when my wife would be back.

I scanned the beach, but it was deserted. The old woman and her dog hadn't walked past yet. No footprints in the pristine sand. In the distance, I observed the long clouds heavy with rain, which seemed to stroke the surface of the water. A storm had been forecast for the afternoon.

I took a deep breath of ocean air and expelled the grime from my lungs. I knew I had to go back to it. I had to start from the beginning and read the entire manuscript again, despite Samuel's advice and Sarah's anger.

I went back inside, sat down, and reached for the pile of pages waiting on the coffee table. Right next to them was a lukewarm cup of coffee. I picked it up, studied the rim and noticed a brown droplet that had dried on the edge. As usual, the stain prevented me from drinking the coffee.

Your strange obsession . . .

I put down the cup as I reread the opening sentence.

The first time David saw Julie was on 12th August 1986. It was so hot that Friday that the grains of sand stuck to his skin.

Chapter 1

Friday

The first time David saw Julie was on 12th August 1986. It was so hot that Friday that the grains of sand stuck to his skin.

The boy had arrived that morning, with his mother and stepfather, and had already got settled in to bungalow 18 of the holiday village in Saint-Hilaire-de-Riez on the Atlantic coast. The same one they occupied every year. In his refreshingly cool room, he had unpacked all his toys and set them up on the Formica table, then put away his clothes in the wardrobe and prepared his beach bag. This small level of activity had left a fine layer of sweat on his forehead, which he wiped away with the back of his hand. It was looking to be a very hot summer. When he'd climbed out of the car, David had noticed that the tarmac was already melting. Now, he quickly put on his swimming trunks, thinking of the roaring waves he had heard as soon as they had parked on Avenue des Mouettes.

The adults immediately opened the shutters in the different rooms, chasing away the peaceful darkness that had been slumbering inside. The light seemed to irritate the dusty sofa, pale walls, and dull linoleum, which the previous occupants had abandoned just an hour before. His stepfather's seasoned eye noticed that the toaster was missing, most likely taken by the previous renters.

"It's not a big deal," said David's mother soothingly. "We'll make the toast in the oven."

"If I say it's a big deal, it's a big deal, okay?" replied her husband.

"Okay."

The holiday bungalow they were renting for the fifth consecutive year was part of a village the factory had acquired in the late 1930s, when paid holidays became the norm. The father of the current

owner—the "old man" as the employees still called him—had seized
an opportunity to buy the former navy barracks to create a holiday
village for his workers. At the time, in 1937, there were nearly four
hundred people working at the factory, and the figure had doubled
during the dark years that followed. The employees—mostly women
during the war—stopped making the usual sheet metal to weld,
hammer, and mould shell casings. Those were the factory's golden
years. After the war, the old man thanked his employees by giving
them a week at the Avenue des Mouettes holiday village in addition
to their usual annual leave. It became a tradition: for one week
every summer, each family could enjoy one of the identical little
bungalows (comprising a kitchen, lounge, bathroom, two bedrooms
and a small patio) located just a few metres from the beach. Only
one building was different from the others: the boss's house. Located
at the centre of the village, it was taller than the bungalows, with
two additional storeys, and its pointed roof resembled a church
steeple. It was also surrounded by a luxuriant garden, which often
played host to huge barbecues during the summer, when the old
man would toast his employees, whom he considered to be friends
or even family.

David helped his stepfather unload the car—a beige Renault 5
which the man worshipped. Then he carried in the bags of food and
boxes filled with bottles of alcohol. The glass made a low clinking
noise as he walked; it was a foreboding sound, like a death knell.

"That should last the week. Have to have something to help me
put up with you!" muttered his stepfather as he gently shut the boot
of his beloved Renault.

One week.

One whole week away from their dingy tower block.

One week to go out at night, go to bed late, run in the sand, eat
ice cream, and hang out with Samuel.

One week of sitting on the beach with something other than the
tired walls of cheap high-rises to look at.

"I remembered your holiday workbook!" his mother called out
from the kitchen.

Great.

One week of dodging the holiday workbook.

Fair enough, *thought David as he put on his backpack.*

He left his room and went into the lounge where his stepfather was already slouched on the sofa with his feet resting carelessly on the coffee table. He gave David a blank stare and then concentrated on the bottle of Kronenbourg in his hand. David went to look for his mother.

"Mum, can I go to Samuel's?" *he asked.*

"Yes, go ahead. Do you remember which house it is?" *she replied with her back to him as she checked the dishes.*

"27," *he said proudly.*

"Behave yourselves, all right? And tell that big brother of his that if he tries to get you to smoke again, he'll be in serious trouble."

"Okay."

"We'll meet you at the beach at eleven thirty. Have you got sun cream in your bag?"

"Yes, Mum! Cream, hat, towel, mask, and flippers. I'm ready for the deep, blue sea!"

"Did you hear me just now?" *she asked as she grabbed a tea towel to dry her hands.* "I remembered to bring your holiday workbook!"

But when she turned back around, David had disappeared.

As if driven away by an ancient curse.

As soon as he left the bungalow, David took off his sandals to walk barefoot on the pavement, which the coastal breeze had covered in sand. The rough, warm surface beneath his feet made him feel safe and happy. He walked all the way down Avenue des Mouettes with his shoes in one hand, and an intoxicating feeling of freedom in the other.

Across from him, the dunes, which marked the end of the tarmac's territory and the beginning of the beach, drew nearer with each step. He could already feel the cool water and hear the thrum of the waves. The air was growing heavier, thickened by the salt and the distinctive smell of seaweed.

Avenue des Mouettes. The only road through the slightly isolated holiday village wound through the bungalows before ending at the beach as abruptly as a flash of lightning disappears from the sky. Its existence became virtual as it vanished beneath the conquering grains of sand, which seemed to be fleeing the beach to make their way inland. David noticed that the ravenous monster had swallowed up even more tarmac than usual this summer.

He promised himself he would check his theory later with Samuel by visiting the "ghost neighbourhood", the line of houses along the dunes that were no longer occupied. Every year, the beach buried these houses a little more. Its grains weighed heavily on the foundations, rising up to and then breaking the windows before flowing inside to take possession of this territory that had once belonged to people. The adults talked about wind and erosion and how much it would cost to demolish the houses. But the children imagined that the sand was made up of tiny soldiers, disciplined troops advancing towards the positions once held by giants armed with hats, sun cream, and crossword puzzles.

David turned left between two conifer hedges. He enjoyed their cool shade and breathed in their unique scent. He picked up the pace as he neared the church-like house. His heart began to race as he glanced despite himself at the heavy front door with its ogival arch. Dried out plants clung desperately to the building with their brittle claws. The relentless sun had fried all life in the abandoned garden some time ago, and loose piles of sand had formed beneath the windows. The paint on the dark wooden shutters was chipped and the tall gate was covered in rust from the salty breeze. Despite the heat, David felt a chill run down his spine and prayed that Samuel had forgotten the pact they'd made the previous year. Because this was where, according to his best friend's older brother, Eléonore Vermont, the wife of the current factory owner, had hanged herself from a beam in the entrance hall a few years earlier.

Many people said she hadn't been all there. They claimed that during the summer barbecues, Mr Vermont Junior's wife would walk aimlessly among the guests, her expressionless face and jerky movements reminiscent of an automated wax doll. Then she would blink, and her gestures and expressions would return to normal. "Lovely party, don't you think?" she would say, without really recognizing the people she was talking to. Her madness had a German-sounding name: Alzheimer's. A kraken trapped in the poor woman's cerebro-spinal sea, where it devoured all of her memories. That's what the adults told themselves when they came home from the parties and, tired or ashamed of their surreptitious jokes, realized that the disease might someday attack their own minds. The employees felt sorry for Paul Vermont and greeted him with a certain sadness when they returned to the factory.

But the version of the story that Fabien liked to tell his brother and David—especially late at night—was quite different. According to him, several people who were more imaginative, more inebriated, or simply too terrified by the science, which clearly implied that this danger could strike down anyone, clung to a version of events steeped in mysticism and folklore. They claimed that the sea breeze had carried the tortured pleas of drowned pirates trapped in their sunken ship to Mrs Vermont's ears. From the depths, the unfortunate souls lamented their fate, mistaking Mrs Vermont for the patron goddess who had once graced the bow of their feared ship. Their relentless calls for help had driven her mad, causing her to hang herself. Ever since her suicide, Fabien always added in a spooky voice, whenever there was a full moon, you could see her ghost wandering the garden, as white and bright as the phosphorescent algae in faraway seas.

David was afraid of Fabien. Not only because—he had to admit it—this story he told them terrified him (he always felt unsteady when he neared the boss's house), but also because of the violence he could sometimes see in the older boy's eyes. Not often, not for long. But his eyes sometimes burned with a ravaging fire that seemed to come to life inside him, especially when he'd been drinking. His words became brutal, full of an anger their whole town knew all too well.

David's mother was very fond of Samuel, but she was also wary of his elder brother. In her opinion, he was just another hoodlum. His stepfather, however, liked him a lot and back at home he occasionally invited him over for a drink. After all, they both worked at the factory. They had that in common. And they both had that same violence within. Enough to come up with a plan and convince other men from the factory to follow them. But David only realized that a few days later.

Samuel opened the door. He was already wearing his backpack. He was slightly taller than David. His ears stuck out a bit, which had resulted in some teasing at school, but his scrappy fists had quickly silenced all those who dared mock him, even the older children.

The two boys greeted one another with a high five and immediately set out back the way David had come. He was relieved when Samuel said nothing as they passed by the haunted house. Maybe his best friend had forgotten their pact . . .

"Isn't your brother here?" asked David as Mrs Vermont's house and madness disappeared behind them.

"He is, he's in his room. He's unpacking and didn't want to be disturbed. He's been acting strange lately."

"Fabien, strange? What's new?!" teased David.

"Yeah, well, let's just say stranger than usual then. He may be a real dick, but he's my brother, and he really has been weird lately."

They took a shortcut along Rue des Galées and the first grains of sand appeared underfoot.

"Did your parents get you a holiday workbook too?" asked David.

"Only your mum would think of that!" laughed Samuel. "My parents don't give a shit. They say I'll just end up working at the factory anyway. Like my dad and brother."

"Did you bring a ball?" David interrupted as they crossed the car park at the end of Avenue des Mouettes.

"Yeah, in my bag. How's your idiot stepdad?"

"Same as usual."

"Do you ever dream of being as strong as him and giving him a beating for a change?"

"Pretty much every night!"

They reached the beach, which seemed wider than the year before. Their feet sunk into the white dune and the reeds brushed against their legs. The boys had been waiting for this all year. They scrunched up their toes in the sand, as if trying to grab on tighter, testing the reality of their happiness. At that moment, the classroom and their bushy-browed teacher, Mr Deleporte, seemed very far away. As did their tower block and the smell of stale piss in the lobby. And the fear of being shut up in one of the flats with a violent adult.

The only thing they felt was immortality. It bubbled through their veins.

There weren't many people at the beach that early in the day. The two friends chose a spot near a rocky outcrop and headed towards it, walking past a woman who was reading a story to a girl about their age. The girl turned around to wave at them. Samuel and David looked down in unison and hurried on, ignoring the small, blonde girl.

When they reached their destination, they sat down on the rocks and stared at the unchanging dance of the sea that stretched out before them.

David glanced back furtively at the girl, who now seemed completely absorbed in the old woman's words.

He didn't know it yet, but that glance would change his life forever.

*

I decided to take a break from reading.

I dragged myself to the kitchen, where I put a capsule into the espresso machine and prepared a cup. Although the sky was grey, and the clouds were reaching down towards the ocean on the horizon, I could feel the sweat on my back.

The pages had been burning my eyes for a week. It was like staring at the sun without any protection. Eventually the reality around me became nothing but abstract shapes and dark spots.

Was I trying to avoid the inevitable? This was the fourth time I'd read this far, but I still hadn't got past chapter seven.

I picked up my cup, checked to make sure a drop of coffee hadn't sullied the porcelain rim, and returned to my armchair to get back to my reading. I now knew the beginning of the story by heart. But I still felt like I had to dig deeper between the words to learn the truth. The old woman still hadn't walked past. Maybe I'd been too absorbed to notice. Or maybe I'd fallen asleep. Sometimes I felt like reality was slipping through my fingers. I stopped combing my hair in the morning. All day I would pace the house looking for something to tie me to reality, smoking cigarette after cigarette. I was unsure when the decay had begun to set in. Monday? Tuesday? More recently?

A slew of questions ran wild through my brain, but not a single answer appeared to ease my uncertainty.

So, I dived back into the manuscript, willing to risk drowning in it as Sarah had predicted.

Little did I know how right she would turn out to be.

Chapter 2

The children basked in their freedom until David's mother and stepfather turned up at the beach. The two boys clammed up during their picnic lunch with the adults. Then they went swimming and played football, letting his stepfather have his own way so that they didn't set him off. After a while, once he'd had his fill of beers and easy victories, the man stopped paying attention to them. David finally started breathing normally again as his good mood returned. He and Samuel talked sport, sang "The Final Countdown" without actually knowing any of the lyrics, dreamed about the Nintendo video game console that was set to launch the following year and was expected to unseat Samuel's Atari 2600 (the rare times Fabien let them play), and spit on their palms to shake on a promise that they would hold their first séance when they got home. Samuel took things even further, suggesting they should leave the television on like in Poltergeist, *to see if spirits really could contact them through the static of the cathode-ray tube.*

Then they lay down on their towels and closed their eyes.

Soothed by the sound of the laughing gulls, the two boys fell asleep as the sun began its descent.

When David woke up, he thought that the female voice he'd heard mumbling to him incomprehensibly as he slept, had escaped his dreams and entered reality. The evanescent memory of the siren from his dream lasted a few seconds, until he opened his eyes and realized where the voice was really coming from.

A silhouette set against the burning disc of the sun was leaning over him. He squinted to block out the glare and recognized the girl

*who had waved earlier, when neither he nor Samuel had been brave
enough to reply.*

*"That really wasn't very nice!" she repeated, her voice thick with
reproach.*

*David propped himself up on his elbows, pulling himself reluc-
tantly out of his lethargy. He looked around for Samuel or his
mother but didn't see either of them. He realized he had no choice,
he would have to confront this girl, who was still staring at him,
waiting for a reply.*

"What? What wasn't nice?" he stammered, his mouth dry.

*"Earlier. I waved to you. You didn't wave back. Auntie says you
should always return a kind gesture."*

*"I . . . We did . . ." he mumbled, trying desperately to put an end
to the unwelcome conversation.*

"And you're a liar too!"

*The girl stared at him with her pale-green eyes. He got lost in
them for a moment. He felt so at home there that it was like being
back in his dream. The shoulder-length blonde hair around her
young face seemed to absorb all the sunlight, turning it an even
prettier shade of gold.*

*"All right, okay. It wasn't nice. I'm sorry," conceded David when
it became clear that he would not have the last word. This freckle-
faced girl wouldn't let it go until he admitted defeat. There are people
like that, people who drink your words and use them as fuel for
future questions. They drain you of all your energy by forcing you
to speak.*

*He sat up, his face red, and began folding his towel, silently
cursing Samuel for disappearing on him. It was as if he'd been
swallowed up by quicksand! His best friend actually had told him
he was leaving, but David had been dozing and had forgotten this
detail. Or maybe the siren and her song from his dream had the
power to make him forget . . .*

*A few metres away, the old woman whom the talkative girl had
called Auntie was watching the scene, an amused look on her face.*

"Are you leaving now?" asked the girl.

"Yes, I have to go home. They'll be waiting for me," lied David.

"Will you come back to the beach tomorrow?"

Part of him told him to say no. This girl would undoubtedly ruin the comfortable silences he and his best friend often enjoyed. And what would Samuel say about a stranger elbowing her way into their precious friendship?

"Yes," he replied, before realizing what he had said.

"I'm Julie," said the girl with a smile.

But David had already turned his back to her and started walking towards the entrance to the beach. It took him a moment to integrate the name the girl had offered up with such ease. Julie. He smiled without knowing why, then felt an urge to turn around to look at her again. He had to admit there was something about her.

On the way back to the bungalow, David found himself repeating her name over and over again. Julie. He whispered it in a cheerful tone, then serious, charming, playful. Each incantation felt like a guilty pleasure. Who did she think she was, anyway? How did she just strike up a conversation with a stranger like that? He didn't think he'd ever seen her before. Did her parents also work at the factory, or was she just a tourist? How old was she? So many questions he wanted to ask her. But that would mean he would have to overcome his shyness and risk exposing the sudden interest she had awakened in him. She would probably laugh and make fun of him. *"No way!"* he exclaimed as he decided to forget about the whole thing. Nevertheless, nothing—neither the smell of barbecued sausages wafting through the air as he passed the Vinçons' bungalow (the best welder at the factory according to his stepfather) nor even the police car driving slowly through the neighbourhood—could chase Julie from his thoughts. He felt like he was sleepwalking as he made his way up Avenue des Mouettes. The sun's final rays peeped out over the horizon and the seagulls' incessant chatter finally quietened. David felt like the summer itself had just changed somehow, taking on an odd, unfamiliar consistency. *"Is this what it means to grow up?"* he wondered without fully understanding why he was feeling both sad and strangely elated.

*

The police car drove by again, but the boy still didn't give it a second thought. Behind the wheel sat a young officer from Saint-Hilaire who had been assigned to the tiny seaside town for the months of July and August. He had been patrolling for over two hours now. His boss had told him to spend the afternoon driving the road from the centre of town to the Twisted Wood campsite. Henri knew the road by heart. He had ridden his bike along it thousands of times during previous summers, when he had still been young and carefree, when he had yet to take on the role of a public servant. It was often to visit girls at the campsite; he couldn't understand a word those pretty foreigners said but their laughter had been enough.

Then he had done his military service, and his uncle had reminded him that duty to country and state was a serious business.

And now he found himself wearing a uniform and a cap, which rubbed against his skin and left ridiculous red marks on his forehead, as he travelled the same road he had travelled all those happy years, except now he was boiling, trapped in the scorching interior of a Renault R4.

No matter how hard he listened, he couldn't hear a single laugh.

And he wouldn't in fact hear another for many years to come.

Chapter 3

When he opened the door to the bungalow, David was greeted by muffled voices, speaking barely above a whisper. The men were in the lounge, sitting around the coffee table, each with a glass in his hand. When they caught sight of him, they all went quiet, as though he had caught them red-handed. Then his stepfather reassured them, "He's just a kid, doesn't understand a thing." Samuel's brother called out, "Hey, brat!", but the rest of them remained silent until David left the room.

David had recognized three of the men as workers from the factory. He wouldn't have been able to conjure up names to go with the faces, but he knew they had been to his flat before. One of them had even given him a book for his birthday once. As he'd read Treasure Island, David had wished that that stranger was his stepfather, rather than the Billy Bones he actually had, who seemed to have stepped straight out of Stevenson's story to make his life a living hell.

As he'd crossed the room with the adults' eyes all focused on him, David had also noticed the man sitting at the far end of the sofa. As soon as he'd realized who it was, he'd lowered his eyes and hurried past.

Red.

The scar.

The sole resident of the "ghost town".

David held his breath until he reached the kitchen. Once safely inside, he opened his eyes and leaned against the wall, still shaking. For a moment, it felt like the wall and the whole house were rocking in the waves like the reeking hold of a slave ship. The feeling slowly dissipated as the men got back to their conversation.

What was Red doing here? If there was one person in the world that David and Samuel tried to avoid, it was him. Of all the adults they knew, all the workers from the factory, Red was the one that scared them the most. He wasn't particularly tall—quite the opposite, in fact. He was rather short compared to David's stepfather. But he was definitely stronger. His thick arms, tense jaw, and steel-blue eyes intimidated everyone who came close. He could already imagine how Samuel would react when he told him that Red had spent the evening at his place. His best friend would shudder at the mere thought of it . . .

He had been too busy trying to chase the image of the vivid scar from his mind to notice his mother who was standing motionless at the sink. She hadn't even seen him come in. Her right hand hung lifeless at her side, holding a cigarette that threatened to drop its neglected ash onto the linoleum. Plates full of snacks for the men sat forgotten on the table, waiting to be taken into the lounge. David realized that she was staring out of the window towards the big house. The building rose straight up into the evening air about fifty metres away. He wondered which version of events his mother believed. Dementia or ghosts. It occurred to him that he'd never heard her mention it. But what really intrigued David was the way she seemed to be studying the house. Those dark walls appeared to have inhaled her entire being. She was literally absent; she had left her body behind and was looking for somewhere to seek refuge, far from the men in the next room.

"Mum, are you all right?" he finally asked.

She blinked. Her hand came back to life. Her body turned away from the sink and she stepped over to the table to tap her cigarette over the ashtray.

"Yes, I'm fine. Home already?"

She seemed surprised to see him. He couldn't help but notice the reproachful tone in her voice. She turned towards him and bent down so that they were both at eye level, as though she were looking in a mirror. David gathered from her tired, red eyes that her reply had been a lie. She wasn't all right. She had given up on fighting *the violence a long time ago. She'd got used to it. She had fed herself so many empty excuses that she had come to accept it. "He's not a bad man" and "Sometimes I deserve it" were placebos she swallowed down to try to block out the truth.*

And it worked.

It worked so well that she didn't even try to protect her son from her sadness any more. She let it show on her tired face.

It came as naturally to her as a smile.

That evening, David realized that beyond a certain limit, adults could no longer lie about their unhappiness. His mother stood back up and let her eyes go vacant as she stared out of the window once more. It felt to David like she didn't want to be there right now, at that moment, with them *in the next room, with those men. As if on cue, their glasses started clinking again. When he realized that maybe she didn't even want to be there with* him, *now, at that moment, he fought to hold back the tears.*

"What are all these people doing here?" he asked, swallowing the lump in his throat.

His mother replied without looking at him, despite the fact that she always scolded David if he refused to make eye contact when ordering bread at the baker's.

"Your stepfather asked some friends over. They have serious things to discuss. It would be best if you went to your room for now. Take some biscuits and orange juice with you. I'll come and get you when they're done."

The boy observed his mother for a moment. The light in her eyes seemed to be going out. He decided to do as he'd been told.

Once the door was closed, he could let his tears flow freely. He lay down on the bed clutching his pillow to his chest. He stayed that way for some time, watching the half-moon rise slowly through the branches of the tall pine outside his window. After a while, he wiped his eyes, nibbled on a biscuit, and thought how glad he was that it wasn't a full moon tonight. If his mother was still staring at the boss's house, he didn't want her to catch a glimpse of the wandering pirate goddess.

Later that night, David woke up. He had dreamed about his

mother and a threatening cloud over her head. She had been in the garden at the big house. Her dress had got caught in the brambles and had been ripped to shreds by the thorns as she made her way towards the ocean, seemingly drawn by underwater voices. He chased the images from his mind by thinking about his plans for the next day: the beach, Samuel, and ice creams sold by the usual vendor, who hauled his cart laboriously through the sand like a reluctant donkey every year.

His stomach growled. He felt around for the plate of biscuits, hoping that there were a few left. But he stopped short when he heard talking in the lounge. He recognized the voices of his "parents". It must have been late. The guests had left for the night. David concentrated on making out what the adults were saying. He thought he heard crying, then a few words here and there—"you're crazy", "that won't change anything", "you could get in big trouble"—but his mother's complaints were met with the burning sound of a slap on the face.

And then another.

Then footsteps.

A door slamming.

The nauseating creaking of the mattress for what seemed like an eternity.

The muffled moaning which got increasingly louder.

Then silence.

A silence as heavy and uncomfortable as a hot night.

So, David, as he often did, sought out positive images to distract himself, images that might help ease his sadness.

And to his great surprise, it was Julie's face that accompanied him until he fell asleep.

Chapter 4

Saturday

The next day, Samuel knocked on David's door.

Already dressed in his swimming trunks and a T-shirt, David was finishing his bowl of cereal alone in the kitchen. He had woken up early, hoping the morning light would help erase the uncomfortable night he had spent. The adults always had a lie-in on holiday. It was barely ten o'clock, but the heat, which filtered into the bungalow through the tiniest gap, slithering like a snake through slits in the doors and windows, already weighed on his movements, slowing him down.

David studied the boss's house as his mother had the previous evening. He lost himself for a moment, hypnotized. A spoonful of cornflakes hovered over his bowl, waiting patiently for him to return to reality. The lawn around the big house had turned yellow. The long blades of grass reached skyward like tiny skewers. The heavy chain bound by a steel lock which barred the front gate gleamed menacingly. All of the ground-floor windows had been boarded up, while the first-floor windows were protected by simple shutters. The summer before, Samuel had suggested they try to get in that way.

"All we'd have to do is reach the first floor. We could climb up the gutter or use a ladder. I'm sure those old shutters would be easy to open."

"Do you really want to visit a haunted house?" David had asked, not feeling very confident about entering the hanged woman's lair in the dead of night.

"Do you really believe those stories? She had Alzheimer's, that's all. Don't listen to my brother. Next year, we're trying it."

"Okay, but I'm bringing my proton pack just in case," David had replied with a smile.

"*Great! I'll make sure to have some garlic and a crucifix on me. You never know.*"

David emptied the rest of his breakfast into the sink. He left his bowl and spoon there too and was just going to prepare his beach bag when he heard the knock on the door. A few minutes later, the two friends were walking briskly down Avenue des Mouettes.

"*You're not talking,*" said Samuel. "*Are you okay?*"

"*Didn't sleep very well,*" said David. "*The heat . . . Nothing like back home on the estate.*"

"*My brother was at your place last night. He came home a bit drunk.*"

"*Yeah, I know. It was some sort of meeting. Guess who else was there.*"

"*I don't know. The hanged woman?*"

"*Very funny,*" replied David, rolling his eyes. "*Red.*" He looked intently at his friend, who stopped in mid-stride.

"*Are you serious?*"

"*I'd never seen him at mine, at least not on holiday. That guy really freaks me out,*" added David.

"*You're telling me!*"

The boys didn't know why they were so afraid. Or rather, they didn't know exactly what about the man scared them. His face? ("*Can you believe those eyes? It's like they never move. They're cold. Like a reptile!*" Samuel had said one day.) His scar? ("*My brother says Red got that scar as a child. His father was drunk and angry. He grabbed the kid's face and broke a bottle to cut his cheek.*") His hair? (In the Middle Ages, redheads were thought to be Satan's envoys, Samuel had read in a history book.)

None of these possibilities, even combined, could explain why he inspired such fear in them. There was something else. Something much more jarring, something that made the boys' stomachs churn each time they caught sight of the man.

It was the adults who involuntarily caused it.

It was their attitude towards him.

Their silence when Red entered a room.

Their shifty eyes whenever he spoke to them in his typically blunt manner.

It wasn't the children's fear that had created the figure of the dangerous, bloodthirsty Red. It was the adults'. The children had noticed more than once that everyone feared him. They were like a pack bowing down to the alpha wolf. Even David's stepfather kept his head down around him. So did Fabien, who had warned his brother one day to steer clear of Red. He hadn't given any reason, but his face was pale. It was a warning, almost a request.

"Do you know what they were talking about?" asked Samuel, curious to know why the adults had gathered together inside instead of enjoying the evening light in the garden.

That was the holiday custom. Aperitifs. Beers and barbecue. The bungalow gardens were never empty. Unless it was raining, in which case the families retreated into their bungalows, like snails in their shells, cursing the weather for ruining their holiday.

"No idea!" David replied quickly. He thought it best to keep the enigmatic phrases he'd overheard from his bedroom to himself.

They set up on the beach in the same spot as the day before. They unfolded their towels, put on their caps, and rubbed sun cream on themselves, as instructed. A flock of sandpipers passed right by them. The birds pecked at the sand for a few minutes, hunting for aquatic insects, then strolled casually along the edge of the water. Their frail-looking legs, barely thicker than twigs, were attached to balloon-like bodies. Their high-pitched whistles blended with the hoarser cries of the grey gulls nesting above the beach in little alcoves in the cliffs. David was particularly wary of these birds. All because of a black-and-white film he'd seen by accident one rainy afternoon. In it, people were attacked by birds of all species—not only at the beach, but also in city centres and in their homes—and fat-bellied gulls were some of the culprits. Ever since, he had kept his distance from their threatening beaks.

The ocean flooded the horizon across from the two boys. The waves seemed stronger than the day before. They made a different sound as they crashed into the sand—louder and more guttural. They seemed more determined, too. As though they aimed to hit the beach as hard as possible and frighten the tourists. But instead the children found it amusing. They leapt happily over the cresting water. Parents pretended the current was pulling them out to sea, and the ocean retreated from the beach, only to try again moments later. Its futile anger would last the entire day. It would not have any respite until the moon appeared.

"Look, there she is again," said Samuel.

He nodded in the direction of the beach entrance and David turned to look. He squinted to filter out some of the aggressive light which made it hard to distinguish the distant shapes. Then he saw her. Julie was walking towards them, her backpack over her shoulder. Behind her, the old woman tried to keep up, red-faced and breathing heavily. David doubted she would succeed and as he watched, she gave in. She dropped her basket not far from the boys, watching as Julie continued towards the water. A few seconds later, the girl stopped right in front of them, put down her bag on the warm sand, pulled out a towel and started spreading it out carefully on the beach.

"That wasn't very nice of you!" she declared once she had finished.

She stood there tall and proud, looking combative in the face of their silence and incredulity. Her fists rested on her thin hips and her blonde hair was tied up in a ponytail, revealing the perfect line of her neck.

The same sentence. Again. David knew there was no point asking what she was talking about. Julie would explain it all once she had laid the foundations for the conversation she was building up all by herself. But Samuel, of course, didn't know any of this.

"What wasn't very nice?" he asked.

Julie turned her emerald gaze from David to Samuel. She seemed annoyed that he was the one to ask the question and sighed deliberately before replying.

"First of all, I waved to you yesterday and neither of you waved back. Then, I talked to your friend. I told him my name, and he just turned his back on me and walked off as if I'd insulted him. That *wasn't very nice.*"

"Oh fair lady," cried Samuel in a theatrical tone as he stood up.

"*Please excuse my friend, he is terribly shy! My name is Samuel and this idiot, the one looking at his toes right now, is David. Pleased to meet you!*"

"*I'm Julie,*" she replied, a serious expression on her face as she shook the hand Samuel held out. "*Is your idiot friend going to shake my hand with his feet, too?*"

David rolled his eyes, wondering if he was already asleep and dreaming the scene before him. Then he stood up in turn and held out his hand, which he wished was a bit less clammy and shaky.

The girl shook it gently, holding on to it for a few seconds.

"*Wonderful,*" she announced. "*Now that we've been introduced, we can be friends!*"

And all three of them sat down.

And all three of them smiled.

Auntie watched the children.

She saw first-hand how they signed an invisible pact without even realizing it. This is how great friendships begin, sealed with a simple smile, *she thought, envying their youth. She saw them stand up in unison and make their way to the water. She heard their laughter over the waves.*

Eventually, her fears evaporated.

Of course she had to be careful. Auntie was acutely aware of that. And she remembered her instructions. But at that moment, she was certain she had made the right decision, despite her initial doubts. The old woman looked away from the ocean, towards the houses on Avenue des Mouettes. He must be watching as well, through a window somewhere. Lurking in the shadows. Was he enjoying the show as much as she was? What exactly did he do after dark? *Auntie never would have asked him directly.* There are voices better left beneath the waves, *she concluded as she turned her attention back to the children.*

Fifteen minutes later, the old woman rifled through her basket to find an apple and the newspaper she had purchased on their way to the beach. She thought for a moment that she might offer fruit and biscuits to the children, but decided it was best not to bother them. In fact, they had gone quiet. All three of them were lying on their backs on their towels, basking in their friendship. She turned directly to the last page of the newspaper to find her beloved crossword puzzle, took out a pen and got to work.

If Auntie had glanced at the headlines on the front page instead, she would have seen a face.

And when she saw that face, she would have been frightened.

Very frightened.

Maybe she would have decided to put a stop to things, to stop believing in a promise. Maybe she would have taken Julie from her friends, providing meaningless explanations and confusing excuses that would go over the girl's head. Or maybe, eager to let Julie have her fun, she would simply have watched over her with heightened awareness, reducing the number of hours they spent at the beach or the length of their after-dinner walk.

One thing was certain: if Auntie had seen the picture on the front page, she would have had the answer to all her questions.

She would have known what he did after dark.

And the answer would have frozen the blood in her veins.

Chapter 5

Tuesday

Two days went by.

The children now did everything together.

They strolled along the beach and Avenue des Mouettes side by side, elbow to elbow, usually with Julie sandwiched between the two boys.

Like a guarded treasure.

They spent most of their time at the beach. A slew of newly arrived tourists had also decided to take advantage of the spot. Parasols sprouted like multicoloured mushrooms, balls rolled between the multitude of towels, and the sun scorched the skin of those who weren't diligent enough with the sun cream.

Though in previous years they had always gone to the beach with David, this year his mother and stepfather made few appearances. Usually his mother spent hours perfecting her tan so that she could make the whole tower block jealous upon returning home, and his stepfather would alternate between racket sports and football matches with his colleagues from the factory.

David thought it was strange that he didn't see them more, but he stopped worrying when he realized that their absence meant he could spend even more time with his two friends.

The three children had fun making up names for the different families who gathered on the beach around them. They mocked some of them, sniggering together when they saw a group trudging through the sand wearing flip-flops with socks. They spent hours like that, promising never to grow up, swearing they would never resemble the objects of their derision. Then, when the beach began to empty, they would leave their spot to look for imaginary treasures beneath the wet sand exposed at low tide. They dug their hands down deep and pulled up seaweed, clams, mussels, and even crabs though they were hoping for gold and precious gemstones ("Maybe we'll find One-Eyed Willy's treasure!").

Julie integrated the former duo with disarming ease. As though she'd always been the missing piece of the jigsaw. In the late afternoon on Wednesday, as the three of them studied their loot in a plastic bucket after going fishing, Samuel decided to ask the question he and David had been pondering since they first met the girl.

"Where are you from?" he asked, still counting the shells.

Julie paused before answering. She wasn't entirely certain that the question had really been asked. Maybe it had simply escaped from her own mind, like an inevitable truth. She was, in fact, surprised that her friends' curiosity hadn't got the better of them sooner. She knew what she had to say.

"Bordeaux," she replied half-heartedly.

"Bordeaux? Is that far?" asked Samuel.

"Not very."

"Do you have any siblings?"

"No."

"So your parents don't work at the factory, then?"

"No," she replied laconically, before correcting herself quickly. "I mean, what factory?"

"Vermont Steelworks. Our parents work there. But it's not in Bordeaux. I'll probably work there one day, too, when I'm older," Samuel explained.

"What about you, David?" asked Julie, trying her best to change the subject. She wanted to run to Auntie, who was sitting not far away.

"I don't know," replied David, who had turned his attention from their catch to the horizon. "'When I'm older' still feels a long way away . . . I don't really want to . . . I'd like to visit other countries."

"A real pirate!" said Samuel with a laugh. "Well, I guess we should chuck all this back. There's no gold here."

Samuel swung the bucket over the water then tossed its contents into the waves and rinsed out the last grains of sand. The three children headed back to their towels. Auntie was packing up; it was time to go home.

"What do your parents do?" Samuel asked.

Here we are, the moment I've been dreading, *thought Julie, who had hoped Samuel had finished with his questions. That was part of the reason why she felt such affection for David (not to mention his eyes, his sensitivity, the world hidden away beneath the surface). He didn't talk much, as though afraid to disturb other people's secrets. He never would have asked that question. He would have relished the silence. Samuel, on the other hand, needed to know. And curious people are always more vulnerable to lies.*

"They're dead," she mumbled.

*

I stood up, suddenly anxious, leaving the pages behind. I lit a cigarette and paced the lounge, fully aware that the sentences which followed would be more and more painful to read.

"They're dead."

I remembered those words. That moment. That indescribable feeling.

The setting sun.

The nearly deserted beach.

The tide rushing out.

The way Mother Nature herself seemed to want to escape what came next.

I could still see Julie's blonde hair blowing in the sea breeze. I only dared glance furtively at it. Its reckless dance evoked a ripped sail on a lost ship. That was burned into my memory, too.

I stepped out onto the patio and experienced the same shivers that I had felt that day. I remembered the sensations that ran through me when she uttered that sentence: I was paralyzed. My entire body froze. And my thoughts with it. Washed up on the beach of a sentence that made no sense to me.

Death is incomprehensible for children; a shadow with no real substance, an anomaly which has no place in a twelve-year-old's imagination. Parents live, separate, disappear without having any contact with their children, but deep down we know they're out there somewhere, they're alive.

To try to understand what Julie was feeling, I had done my best to imagine my mother was dead. But I couldn't do it. So, I just stared out at the ocean. And the waves washed in and out, like the hands of a dusty old clock marking time in a lonely room.

And now, looking out at those same waves, I knew exactly how she had felt. My mother had fought her cancer for a few years, but she had lost. During her final days, when her face became as white and vaporous as the smoke from the cigarettes which had slowly nourished the disease, I saw that look again, a look I hadn't seen in years. The look I had glimpsed when I had come home from the beach to find the men talking in the lounge.

The resignation I had seen in her eyes that night was a reflection of the same feeling expressed by Julie four days later.

Resignation to what I began calling "first deaths" as I cried in my room later that evening. I realized at that point in my childhood that small parts of us were constantly dying. That suffering which never fully healed would wear on the body and mind until the victim found themselves in the morgue or at the end of a rope. Life was full of these first deaths. They made ghosts of us all. Mrs Vermont had become one. The slow but steady disappearance of her memory was her first death. It wore her down until she hung herself.

As for my mother, she had died a little every time my step-father hit her or insulted her. She had died even more when he went for me. And the events of the summer of 1986 would cling to us like an aggressive disease, and would go on to infect the rest of our lives.

I sighed heavily before lighting another cigarette. In the distance, stringy clouds seemed to seep down to the surface of the sea. It was about to rain. The wind picked up, chasing me inside. On the other side of the glass, safe from the squalls and from Julie, my thoughts turned to Sarah, my only anchor in this approaching storm. What was she doing? When would she come home? I felt an intense urge to call her, to apologize, to hold her close. I picked up my mobile and stared at it for a moment. Behind me, the first drops struck the French windows. The gentle pitter-patter quickly turned into a battering downpour. The wind's discreet murmur became a mournful wail, surrounding the house and trying to force its way in.

I knew that if I begged Sarah to come home tonight, I wouldn't be able to finish the pages. In fact, the first thing she would do upon returning would be to burn them and make me promise to forget all about them. I couldn't do that. I had to continue. I had to relive my "first deaths" in order to finally understand. I put the phone down and returned to my armchair. Outside, the tormented sea was the same grey hue as the sky. The subtle tone-on-tone made it difficult to distinguish one from the other, as if the two elements had decided to become one. The image was a perfect copy of the Hiroshi Sugimoto photograph that Sarah had purchased for a ridiculous price at an exhibition in Paris. We had organized a weekend in the capital (I had agreed to emerge from my bubble for two days to celebrate the release of my third novel) and we had visited all of the most prestigious galleries on the hunt for a piece to "bring a little warmth to this big heap of metal and glass" as she put it. As soon as Sarah saw it, she'd fallen in love with it. As she studied the pearl-grey hues of the photograph entitled *Ligurian Sea,* she uncovered a myriad of poetic metaphors: loss of your bearings, the passage of time, a perfect melding of two beings . . . I simply nodded and agreed while looking in vain for a price tag which wasn't there. After sharing the Japanese artist's biography, the gallery owner finally whispered the price of the work (tens of thousands of euros). Sarah shot me a determined look, designed to quell any opposition to the idea, and had said simply, "It would be perfect in our bedroom".

Thinking back to the photograph (which no longer attracted my gaze as it had in the weeks following its purchase), I thought that this disturbing yet poetic grey vision may have been what

Mrs Vermont had seen as she wandered over Avenue des
Mouettes towards the shore. I imagined her walking away from
her house, oblivious to her surroundings, in a desperate attempt
to locate the pleas that kept her trapped between two worlds,
trapped in a mysterious place where the voices of the dead
mixed with those of the living, where the ghostly horizon no
longer separated the sea from the sky.

"Don't be an idiot," I told myself, trying to brush aside the
childish thoughts. "She hung herself to escape her disease. This
is no time to start believing in ghost stories!"

I returned to my reading, determined to finish it as quickly
as possible, so that I could rid myself of my growing fear and
assuage my morbid curiosity. I glanced at the gloomy seascape
one last time, certain in the knowledge that the wind would
soon turn and make way for a rainbow on the horizon.

I quickly regretted that thought, though. Because I remembered that back when pirates roamed the waves, a rainbow
wasn't only a symbol of fair weather.

It was also believed to be a bridge between the world of the
living and the world of the dead.

*

*The light drained from Julie's eyes as she told the boys about her
parents' car accident nine years earlier. "I wasn't with them. I was
waiting to be picked up from my aunt's house. I don't remember
anything about them. Their faces, their voices, nothing."*

*She had lived in Bordeaux ever since, with her aunt, a wealthy
woman who sent her on holiday with Auntie, their housekeeper,
since she couldn't get away herself.*

*The three children sat side by side with their feet in the waves
watching the sun drown in the sea. David felt a lump growing in
his throat as he listened. He kept quiet, noticing that Julie's foot
was almost touching his, and that a grain of sand near her ankle
shone brighter than the others in the dying sunlight. Each of the
children would have liked for the moment to last forever.*

Then Samuel broke the silence and told his own story. It wasn't that he really wanted to, but he knew that David would never speak up on his own. And Samuel felt it was urgent to speak, to put a plaster over Julie's painful words. So he talked about his brother, about his violence and his passion for beer. Then about his parents, who only saw one possible future for him: one filled with machinery and oil-stained hands. He talked about the factory, too, where almost all of the male members of his family worked, and a few of the women as well. He also told a few anecdotes that made their new friend smile again, including the story of the night when he and David had snuck out to go to the arcade at the Twisted Wood campsite a little further up the coast. Luckily, his brother had already passed out drunk and hadn't heard the boys' clumsy attempts to open the bedroom window. When that had failed, they had made their way to the front door, but Fabien was lying right next to it on the sofa, blocking the way. In the end, they had resorted to the toilet, where, with a bit of gymnastics and a lot of muffled laughter, they had managed to wriggle out of the tiny window. He described the multicoloured lights, the video games, the pinball machines, the loud music, the pretty girls who were too old for them, and the smell of candyfloss as though he was a pirate describing a legendary treasure.

"We could do it together," suggested Julie, happy to move on to a more uplifting subject.

"Do what?" asked David, still staring at the bright grain of sand.

"Sneak out! To go to the arcade! We only have four days left together, and I want to see the lights, too!"

"I don't know if—"

"Come stay the night at my place," she continued. "Auntie falls asleep early in the evening. She takes pills. She sleeps so deeply that she often spends the whole night in her armchair and not even the TV wakes her up!"

"That's a good idea!" exclaimed Samuel. "She's right! How about tomorrow? My brother is going to yours, David. He told me this morning. If he comes home as drunk as last time, he won't even realize I'm gone. He never comes to check on me in my room anyway. Tell your mum you're sleeping over at mine. She'll say yes."

David thought it over for a few minutes, ignoring his friends and their enthusiasm. He had made up his mind as soon as Julie had suggested her plan, but he loved letting Samuel stew. And despite their many years of friendship, Samuel still fell for it.

"I'm not sure—"

"Come on David!" Samuel urged. "We're on holiday!"

"Yes, but . . ."

"I have enough pocket money for us to try all the new games!" said his best friend, upping the ante.

"I don't know."

"Space Harrier, Bubble Bobble, Out Run, Arkanoid!"

"Come on David," Julie chimed in, nudging his shoulder. "Don't be a scaredy cat. It's just a teeny white lie."

David decided it was time to stop acting. "All right, let's do it," he said eventually, eliciting a shout of joy from his best friend.

As for David, he felt a strange warmth wash over him when he noticed that the bright grain of sand was now so close it was touching him.

April 1986

Paul Vermont sat down at his desk.

Ever since his accountant had presented bankruptcy as the best solution for the factory, he had spent every sleepless night trying to understand, trying to glimpse a glimmer of hope through the thick, gloomy veil of the inevitable. His meetings with the various banks confirmed his predictions: though it was supposed to remain a secret until September at least, there had been leaks, and rumours were running wild. He had already met with the staff representative and reassured him with soothing lies. Unfortunately, he could not employ the same strategy with the accountant's figures. And the piece of paper he now held in his hands was proof that the rumours had not been quashed. Quite the contrary—they were spreading like wildfire. Every time he walked through the factory, Paul noticed more and more suspicious glances.

The people in the village were simple folk. Geography, history, and economics had conspired to shape the attitude of these residents, imbuing them with remarkable integrity. It was a far cry from the superficiality of the big cities where the people held their heads up high in open defiance of the sun and the misfortune of the rural regions. Here the people kept their heads down, studying the earth beneath their feet, knowing it was far from prosperous. Sometimes they spit on it, mumbling curses, desperately searching the sediment for a seed of hope. And that's what the boss had given them a few years earlier when he had taken over the factory. The employees had loved him for it. He had made it possible for them to hold their heads high by giving them jobs and a reason to get up in the morning, by putting a sparkle of pride back in their eyes. By giving them their chance to defy the sun.

One last summer, thought Paul Vermont.

The factory was empty. The working day had ended a while ago and the timecards had all been punched. Paul liked staying late. Even more so recently. The factory was different at night, like a slumbering beast. The smells were the same, and the huge machines looked just as powerful, but now silence reigned. He imagined it was like the calm after the storm of a great battle, like the spontaneous truces during which enemies could bury their dead without risking their own lives. It was a deafening silence, one that the employees, his foot soldiers, would trample at dawn the next morning.

The director turned the pages. He compared the figures. Added up the bills. Checked on the few orders left to fill. The sun was setting slowly behind the large window. He took in its beauty for a moment, the numbers dancing through his mind like Shakespearian witches.

Once again, he unfolded the strange letter he had received that morning. He reread it, his brow furrowed and fists clenched. Who could have written such a thing? Who already knew? Paul wasn't easily intimidated. He had lived his whole life under pressure. Starting with when he had first taken over the factory from the old man. At that time, many people thought he would drive the company into the ground within the first few months. Suppliers had tried to up their prices, employees asked for raises, and a competitor threatened that the factory would be wiped off the map within months if he did not accept his takeover . . . Then again when the market crashed and steel from Eastern Europe had begun to flood the market. Paul Vermont had been forced to fend off the banks and his accountant, who said he should lay people off. Last but not least, there had been his wife's suicide to contend with, and the weight of his guilt which had almost buried him for good.

All in vain.

Until now.

He closed his eyes for a moment. The memory of the smell of fresh seaweed suddenly assaulted his senses. Another sun shone in another place, above the holiday bungalows, above a house that looked like a church. His right hand moved away from the calculator and mimed opening an invisible gate. He could feel the rough grains of sand under his work boots. Paul strode up the path and across the garden to the building everyone else called "the boss's house". His feet climbed the wooden steps. The heart-warming sound of children playing—catching balls and throwing kites high into the air—rose over the crashing of the waves. He neared the ebony door with its ogival arch and opened it. He knew what he would find inside, but he did it anyway. Paul gazed down. His arrival heralded a whirlwind of dust specks and grains of sand rolled lazily across the parquet floor. He didn't want to look up. But in this dream house, he did. He caught sight of his wife's feet, swaying in the air as she hung from the thick beam.

"Boss, I locked the doors and . . . Boss?"

Red had just stepped into the office.

He was the only person who was allowed in without knocking. He pretended not to see the tears rolling down Paul Vermont's face. He put the keys on the desk as he did every evening, after checking all of the doors and putting the factory's huge ovens to sleep for the night. Faced with his boss's silence—he didn't dare call him a friend; they were both too disillusioned to believe in such things—he decided to leave without another word. Besides, no explanation was necessary. Franck knew what caused the tears. He had been standing next to Paul when he had found his wife's body.

He had untied her from the beam.

As he placed his hand on the doorknob, however, his boss finally spoke. "Summer is nearly here, Franck. Do you remember your promise?"

Chapter 6

Wednesday

The next morning, David woke up around ten o'clock—by this time he was usually knocking on Samuel's door.

He had had a restless night.

When he had come home from the beach the day before, he had hugged his mother close, holding her so tightly that she couldn't help but worry.

"Are you all right?" she asked when he quietly cuddled up next to her. He kept his face pressed firmly to her stomach, as though, if he got close enough, he might find a way out of this world where parents die and back into the reassuring sanctuary that had kept him safe for nine months.

When he finally sat up, his mother kissed his forehead, chasing away his sadness. "Barbecue tonight. Go and have a shower and I'll get your food ready."

They ate dinner in silence. David was eager to leave the table. All he wanted was to be alone. Alone with the memory of his foot touching Julie's. Alone with the memory of her joy when he agreed to their upcoming adventure. Alone with his excitement about the three of them heading for the twinkling lights of the arcade.

He left the adults in front of the television.

A nightmare.

In the boss's house, where thick flames devoured the walls.

David was standing across from the floating corpse, which smiled to see him there amid the fiery storm. The skin of her bare feet began to blister from the heat. But she kept smiling, swaying slowly at the end of her rope, staring unblinkingly at him. Sheets of paper flitted through the air all around him. On each one, the same photocopied face was decomposing, writhing, and curling in on itself before bursting into flames and dissolving into a thin layer of dark ash. "Listen to the ghostly whispers," said Mrs Vermont through dry, cracked lips dripping with blood.

David woke up in a sweat, short of breath, with his hair clinging to his feverish forehead. The sun was already coming up behind the branches of the tall pine. He couldn't decide if he wanted to scream or cry for a few minutes until he finally pulled himself together. "Shut the fuck up," he said, hoping the words would exorcise the images that were still drifting through his mind. He couldn't escape the face from his nightmare—not the hanged woman, although she was terrifying enough to haunt him throughout his adolescence, but the other, younger face printed on the pieces of paper. He felt like he'd seen it before, somewhere besides in his dream, somewhere in the real world, but he couldn't put his finger on exactly where.

He stood up and tugged on his swimming trunks and a T-shirt, trying to convince himself that he was mistaken. *Is there a passageway—like the pirates' rainbow but bleaker and colder—that leads from reality to our nightmares? And worse still, could the creatures locked away in our deepest fears ever use it to go in the opposite direction and claw their way to reality?*

David went to the toilet and then into the kitchen for breakfast. He immediately realized that his mother wasn't there. He couldn't explain it, but as soon as he left his room, he could sense that she wasn't in the house. He found his stepfather in the same trancelike position adopted by his mother the day before. Leaning against the stove with a cigarette in his hand, he was staring at the tall, dark house and didn't move or speak when his stepson said good morning.

David grabbed his favourite bowl from the sink, rinsed it out, and poured in the cereal and milk. He began eating in silence, making sure not to swallow too loudly, since he knew his stepfather hated that. Three spoonfuls later, the adult finally spoke.

"Your mother is crazy. You know that, right?"

David didn't answer. It wasn't really a question. This wasn't the first time his stepfather had spoken to him like this. He knew what *to do. Ignore him. Dive down deep below the sea to keep from hearing the whispers of the living.*

"If you want to become a man someday," continued his stepfather, "you'd better listen to me, not her. Women make babies, not men."

David hunkered down, returning to his own world. He thought about Julie, the arcade and its multicoloured lights. They kept the lethal flames at bay, the flames constantly kindled by the man in front of him.

"Do you hear me, boy?"

This was a real question. He'd better answer.

He'd better leave the depths for a second and come up for air ...

"Yes," he replied meekly.

"Your mother is crazy. You understand?"

"Yes."

"She's a bloody nutjob who'll probably hang herself like old lady Vermont if I don't look out for her," stated his stepfather as he finally dragged his eyes away from the boss's house.

David stopped eating and clutched his spoon so tightly that his knuckles turned white. His stepfather's violence was palpable and David knew that this discussion had one purpose only: offloading that violence. Even onto an innocent boy. Especially onto an innocent boy.

"What did you hear the other day when my friends and I were in the lounge?" he asked, stubbing out his cigarette in an ashtray that hadn't been emptied for days.

"Nothing," replied David.

"That's for the best. I don't like snoops. If you did hear something and you mention it to anyone, you'll be in a world of hurt. Got it?"

"Yes, but I didn't hear anything."

"That's all right, then!"

His stepfather started towards the lounge. As he passed the table, David dropped his spoon. His hand was starting to hurt but watching him go and the prospect of being free of his violence made the pain almost enjoyable. Unfortunately, his stepfather wasn't done with him yet. He stopped in the doorway and turned back towards David.

"Who's your new girlfriend?" he inquired casually.

The flames grew stronger. They burned the walls and the kitchen table, filling the air with the smell of charred wood and melted plastic. As soon as his stepfather mentioned Julie, the air became unbreathable.

"She . . . She's not my girlfriend," David protested.

"Have you kissed her?"

"Stop it."

"Have you touched her boobs?"

"Shut the fuck up!"

He only realized what he'd said after the fact. But this time the magic words could not exorcise the demon in the room. The result was quite the opposite. His stepfather moved swiftly. David felt his cheek connect, not with the thin, supple ends of his fingers, but with his stepfather's thick, heavy palm. The blow sent the boy reeling, his ears ringing like a kettle forgotten on the stove. He could taste blood mixed with chocolate. In a daze, he slowly recovered as the man stood tall and dark across from him, like the house outside.

"Don't ever speak to me like that again. Or next time I'll close my fist. And clean up all this shit!"

David looked to where his stepfather was pointing. Milk and cereal had spilled over the edges of his bowl. Milky tears holding bits of chocolate cereal dribbled over the lip and down to the base. When David picked up the bowl to take it to the sink, there was a perfect circle underneath. Before rinsing it, he studied it for a few seconds.

It was his favourite bowl.

An adult would see nothing but a white dish with a brown monkey swinging through the trees on the side. But for him, it was the latest gift from his mother. She had secretly collected enough cereal tokens to order it. Then, one morning, she had carefully placed it next to the orange juice, and then acted like nothing was out of the ordinary. David had paused when he saw the bowl, which he had only ever asked for once, certain that no one had been listening. But this bowl was proof. Proof that his mother still listened to him. The immaculate plastic bowl meant that everything was intact, that *his mother's love for him hadn't been diminished by his stepfather's presence. He had thanked her earnestly and held her close, just like he had a month later when he came home from the beach after Julie told him about her parents' deaths.*

But now this same bowl was no longer proof of her love. Obscene streaks had disfigured the monkey's happy face.

David turned away from the sink and walked towards the bin. He gently placed the bowl inside and stared at it briefly, etching into his memory this symbol of a perfect moment irreparably damaged.

He had no idea then that the trauma of this scene would remain with him for the rest of his life, rearing its ugly head every time he poured himself a cup of coffee . . .

3

Tuesday, 22nd August

This time, it was the thunder that distracted me from my reading. A gloomy cracking sound, even more threatening than the shrieking wind from earlier, echoed through the sky.

I didn't have any clear memories of the incident with the bowl. And it had never occurred to me that my obsessive avoidance of stained coffee cups might have a concrete explanation. The slaps, the insults, and the loneliness had been public knowledge since the publication of my first book. The author of these pages must have simply taken bits and pieces of the violence from my childhood and copied them here. Nevertheless, though I wasn't sure it was true, I also couldn't say with any certainty that things hadn't happened like that. And since, for the moment, everything I had read seemed to be faithful to reality, there was no reason to assume the description of that morning was any different. I had undoubtedly forgotten certain things over the years—a fact that troubled me. What other truths would I uncover in the following pages? What ghosts from my past might emerge from the ocean?

I looked up to watch the storm and immediately felt a pain shoot up the back of my neck like an electrical shock. My cervical vertebrae were not pleased about having been nervously hunched over the pages for so long. I was rolling my head to loosen my muscles and joints when my phone rang. I jumped up—another shock of pain made me groan—hoping to answer and hear Sarah's voice (because it had to be her, she was on her way, she was coming home and the storm would die down as I opened the door to take her in my arms).

I had my apologies all ready for Sarah, but it was Samuel who spoke.

"How far have you got?" he asked.

That was it. No explanation and no croissants. As if we'd seen each other just minutes before.

"Christ, is that all you have to say? After a whole week?"

"Right, sorry. I needed to check in," said Samuel, eager to get the unwanted topic out of the way.

"The signing in Paris went well if you're interested," I said bitterly.

"Come on, it's not like you're new to all this. Did you want me to hold your hand and wait for you outside? So, how far have you got?"

Sometimes I longed for our simple, innocent childhood discussions. Especially when our exchanges grew tense, when one of us had to make concessions to keep things from going off the rails. Most of the time, I was the one to give in. But sometimes it was Samuel who relented.

"I'm on chapter six," I replied.

"Good, very good," he said with a sigh, clearly relieved.

"What's good about that?" I asked, feeling anger swell within me like the storm outside. "Do you think it's good that reading these pages has upset me to the point that I can't sleep? Do you think it's good that Sarah has left because reliving all this has kept me from living in the present? And how about the fact that I'm torturing myself trying to understand why we were unable to protect her? Bloody hell, Samuel, go on, please tell me what's so good about all this!"

I hadn't just spoken the words. I had shouted them. From my conscience. From my gut. And the questions weren't solely addressed to my best friend, who remained silent for quite some time, seemingly unsure of how to respond. They were questions for Julie. For my mother. For the lights at the arcade, the indifferent sun, and the ghost of the hanged woman in the house I dared not look at. I had just hurled my suffering in the faces of all those who had touched my existence, and my pleas had been met with an absence of sound, not even an echo. I suddenly felt exhausted and terribly alone. I felt absurd staring into the void of so much silence.

"I understand, David," Samuel finally replied. "I understand because I was there, too, and I don't know where this is taking us either . . . But I need you to promise me something."

"What?" I mumbled as I looked for my pack of cigarettes.

"Promise me you'll wait for me before reading the last chapter, chapter twelve."

"What? Wait for you to read it? What's this about? Why should I wait?" I raged.

"Because you'll need an explanation. And I'd rather give it to you myself. Tomorrow morning. I'll come by tomorrow morning. That's why I haven't called since Monday. I had to go back there, after reading my last chapter."

"What are you talking about?"

I felt empty. There were still no answers, and now there were even more questions to add to the list.

"Well, it seems only one chapter differs in our versions," explained Samuel.

"How do you know? We compared our texts on the phone last time."

"Yes, but we only compared the first pages, where you were the main character."

"And?"

"And in the final chapter, *I'm* the protagonist. Chapter twelve explains why I'm 'the silent man'."

Shit. I had been so absorbed by the chapters that I had forgotten all about the preface. The deaf man, the silent man, and the blind man. More mysteries. The guy who wrote this really gave it his all.

"So, you went back there?"

"Yes, I went back to where we grew up. I went back because I thought I knew who had sent us the text. The old factory is still there, you know. Abandoned and falling apart, but still there."

"Who did you go to see?" I asked impatiently.

"A ghost. But I didn't know that until I got there."

"Jesus, could you knock it off with your cloak and dagger bullshit?"

"Not until you've read the last chapter," Samuel replied firmly. "That's when you'll want answers. And I'm the only one who can give you any. So read the rest and wait for me tomorrow morning. Trust me, it's in the best interest of everyone involved."

Then he hung up. It took me several minutes to realize that by ending our call, he had given in this time, protecting our friendship from a potentially damaging conversation.

When I put the phone down, I realized my hands were unusually clammy.

Last Monday, when I had first discovered what these pages held, my first instinct had been to call the police. A childish, idiotic reflex, like a little boy throwing himself into an adult's arms for protection from the monsters under his bed. We've all done it. But the monsters always come back. What would I have said to the officer taking my call? That an unknown person had disturbed me by unearthing my past? That I felt like someone had broken the lock on my mind to free memories I had worked hard to forget over the past thirty years? That I, the writer, would like them to investigate a stranger for writing about what I myself had described—albeit in a vaguer and more metaphorical way—in all of my books? They would laugh in my face. *It was bound to happen given the way you plaster your private life all over the pages of your books. But let me know if a reader kidnaps you and takes you to a remote cabin in the mountains!*

So, I decided against it. I decided to try to figure it out myself.

I glanced at the clock on the wall and realized lunchtime had come and gone and I hadn't eaten a thing. I dragged myself to the fridge where I grabbed the ingredients for a sandwich (tomato, lettuce, cold chicken, mayonnaise) and placed them all on the kitchen island.

"Wait for him to read the last chapter! Yeah right!" I fumed. "As soon as I've finished eating, I'll read the rest, and then I'll burn it all and call Sarah!"

Of course, I didn't do any of that.

Well, not exactly.

Chapter 7

At eight thirty that evening, after kissing his mother goodbye and carefully avoiding his stepfather, David left the bungalow for Samuel's house. In his backpack he'd placed a torch, a pair of pyjamas, his wallet, and his things for the beach the next day. The plan they'd made on the beach earlier that day was simple: wait for Auntie to fall asleep in front of the television, then climb out of the window in Julie's room and head for the Twisted Wood arcade. Julie said they could even bunch up cushions and clothes under the covers, like she'd seen in films. Just a trick in case Auntie woke up and decided to come and check on them on her way to bed. "But she never does. She goes straight from the sofa to her bed," she explained.

"It's going to be amazing, you'll see," promised Samuel. "Usually we go with my big brother, but this way we'll have total freedom!"

"Shush," scolded Julie, nodding discreetly towards Auntie, who was just a few metres away on the beach. "She may sleep like a baby, but she has very sensitive ears when she's not snoring!"

"And the biggest pair of boobs I've—"

"Stop it!" Julie replied with a laugh, trying to place her hand over Samuel's mouth.

"Look over there," David interrupted; he had been silent until then, still shaken by what had happened at breakfast.

"What, more socks and sandals?"

"No. Look . . ."

Not far from them, a man and a woman were making their way up the beach, stopping for a few minutes at each occupied towel, like vendors selling snacks. But instead of handing over bags of caramelized peanuts, the visitors crouched down to converse unsmilingly with the tourists. Then they handed them a piece of paper before moving on, their heads held low, towards the next parasol. The children watched them in silence. They looked back and forth between the people reading the flyer received just seconds before and those who pretended to be busy (one couple even hurried into the water to seek refuge in the waves to avoid being approached). David couldn't help but notice that they seemed to leave an icy atmosphere in their wake. The tourists' faces fell as they looked down at their pieces of paper, their features frozen by an unseen power. Then, once the couple had got far enough away, the ice statues came back to life, quickly putting the flyer down—out of sight, out of mind. Some of them even crumpled it up, as though they feared it might somehow contaminate them. If the couple noticed, they didn't seem offended. They simply continued their work. Slowed by the sand, their bodies clearly weighed down by some invisible force, they only paused occasionally to drink from a water bottle stored in the man's backpack. When they did, they lifted their eyes, reddened from sweat and sand, up from the ground to take in everyone around them, the people enjoying their holidays. But what they saw must not have been to their liking, because as soon as they'd swallowed they put the lid back on the bottle with a frown and returned to their trek, their heads bowed once more.

The woman was the one who spoke to the children. The man stood behind her. But Julie saw tears running down his cheek. Maybe it's just sweat, *she tried to reassure herself without understanding why she felt the need to explain it away in the first place.*

"Hello children, don't be afraid. I've just come to give you something," said the woman.

She looked like she hadn't slept in weeks. Her wrinkled clothing, exhausted features, and empty expression clashed with her gentle voice. She knelt down across from them and paused for a moment as her eyes met Julie's. No one spoke. The children could feel the people around them staring. David thought that this unwelcome feeling of being the centre of attention must be much like the one experienced by Mr Vermont's guests at his legendary barbecues. He realized that the awkward feeling that sent a tingle down the back of his neck and left his mouth dry was a perfect replica of the discomfort Mrs Vermont's illness created in all who crossed her path. It seemed so similar that he almost expected to hear a flood of insults and nonsense pour out of the woman's mouth. But it wasn't madness which spoke that day, though it was already present in the woman's gaze, it was pain. A primitive, animalistic suffering.

"It's my daughter," mumbled the ghost the mother had become. "She hasn't been seen since Friday. I miss her. If you see her, please tell her to come home or call this number. Her name is Emilie. Will you help us?"

"Yes," Julie replied shyly.

Then she instinctively reached up and took the flyer the woman held out. David stared at his new friend. The woman had the same blonde hair as her. He realized then how strange the scene was: Julie, who had lost her parents, across from a mother who had lost her daughter. It was like looking into a mirror that reversed reality. He felt an urge to protect Julie, to tell this woman and her misfortune that they had no place here in their summer. But as anger coloured his cheeks, the woman stood up and joined her husband and they trudged on towards a couple sitting further down the beach. The children watched them go, feeling hypnotized by their presence, captivated by the sadness that emanated from the bereft parents.

"Jesus," said Samuel. "That's freaky."

"It's the picture we've seen all over town," said David when he recognized the face from his nightmare.

"This must be why we've seen so many police cars around," added Julie.

The children had all noticed the photographs. Though none of them had broached the subject, they had all seen them. There was one taped to the newsagent's window near the roundabout. Others were stapled to the wooden electrical poles along Avenue des Mouettes. Still more had landed in the car park, where they fluttered about in the sea breeze. The hundreds of copies of the blonde girl's portrait added a chill to the summer air.

"Maybe she ran away," suggested David.

And his two friends clung to that possibility with him. They convinced themselves that in just a few hours, Emilie would go home and hug her parents in her thin arms, crying out childish excuses. And the summer would be joyful once more. Frisbees would fly through the air, sandcastles would face the assault of the waves, and the three children would watch the horizon, promising never to grow old.

But, then, Samuel—as always—said out loud what Julie and David had decided to ignore.

Something so blatantly obvious that it would leave them feeling out of sorts for the rest of the afternoon.

"Julie, it's crazy how much you look like that missing girl."

Chapter 8

At eight thirty, David headed to his friend's bungalow. The evening sky was swathed in an orangey-yellow veil, as though benevolent fires were dying down in the distant clouds. When he reached the boss's house, he made a run for it, carefully avoiding the shadow of the building, which stretched across the pavement, its gabled windows creating claws on the ground that eagerly awaited their chance to rip his size-three trainers to pieces.

Once he reached Samuel's house, the pair waited for his older brother to leave before making their way to Julie's.

"What are they doing at your place, anyway?" asked Samuel.

"No idea," replied David. "All I know is that my mum doesn't seem very happy when they all come over."

"I don't know what they're up to either, but my brother is really uptight. He doesn't even come to the beach any more."

Julie smiled broadly when she opened the door. "I thought you might wimp out. That wouldn't have been very nice. Come in, I'll introduce you to Auntie."

Auntie was sitting in an armchair in the lounge watching TV. She smiled at the two boys, who didn't dare step into the room.

"Come in, boys, come in. I don't bite, I promise," she urged.

Samuel pushed David forward.

"You must be David," said the old woman as she held out a hand that must have been twice as big as the boy's.

"Yes. I'm very pleased to meet you."

"Oh, so polite! As am I, young man, I've heard so much about you!"

David liked her right away. Her kind face, bright eyes, and even her strange hair style gave him a warm feeling. She sees children differently, not like other adults, *he thought without realizing exactly what that meant.*

"*And you, Samuel, you're not usually so shy, are you?*"

"*Just saving the best for last,*" he announced, pushing his best friend aside. "*This moment will go down in history, I'm certain of it!*" Then he shook Auntie's hand with a theatrical bow.

"*Ah, that's more like it!*" she replied with a laugh.

Julie watched the scene happily. They were the first holiday friends she had ever introduced to Auntie. She had fought hard, begging and laying the charm on thick, to get her to let them stay the night.

"*Are you hungry?*" asked the old woman.

"*No, thank you,*" replied the three children at once.

"*Very well, then, get out of my sight,*" she joked with a comical frown. "*My show's about to start!*"

The three friends gathered in Julie's room to wait patiently for Auntie to fall asleep. They opened the bags of sweets each of them had brought, checked their torches, and counted their money piled up in the middle of the rug.

"*Do we have enough?*" asked Julie.

"*Fifty-seven francs and eighty cents,*" replied David. "*That's enough for at least two hours at the arcade.*"

"*Unless you're up for a boss battle,*" teased Samuel.

At nine thirty, Julie opened her door a crack and listened, then snuck out to make sure Auntie was sleeping. Samuel and David waited, their stomachs full of sweets. They didn't dare speak. They stared at the door, hoping with each passing second that their friend would put an end to their anticipation with a thumbs up that meant the time had come to hit the road. It felt like they had been waiting for hours. Unable to bear it any longer, Samuel broke the silence.

"*What the hell is she doing? Did she decide to watch TV or what?*"

"*Shush! Quiet!*" urged David.

"*Did you see them?*"

"*What are you talking about?*"

"*Auntie's boobs! When she shook my hand, they nearly hypnotized me!*"

"*You're such a pain,*" *complained David.* "*Keep your voice down! And no, I didn't notice them.*"

"*Of course you didn't . . . You never see anything. You never hear anything either,*" *added Samuel enigmatically.*

"*Why do you say that?*"

"*You know the story of the sirens in* The Odyssey, *right? Mr Deleporte read it to us in class.*"

"*Yeah, so?*"

"*Well, they wouldn't have needed wax earplugs for you!*"

"*I don't understand . . .*"

"*I'm saying you are deaf to the song of love! Julie has a crush on you, and you don't even know it! Haven't you noticed the sweet little voice she uses when she's talking to you? 'David, oh David'. Oh! And Auntie: 'Daaaavid, I've heard soooo much about you!'*"

"*What? What are you even talking about? You're nuts! We're just friends, nothing more.*"

"*Yep, you really are deaf,*" *concluded his friend.* "*Poor Julie, all that effort for nothing.*"

As if by magic, when Samuel said her name, Julie reappeared and gave not one but two thumbs up, then quietly shut the door behind her.

"*We're good, she's asleep. Until tomorrow morning at least. Let's go,*" *she said.*

"*Wait,*" *David said, clearly worried,* "*are you sure she won't wake up?*" *His cheeks were unusually red.*

"*I'm sure. The only reason she ever wakes up is for a drink of water. That's why there's always a little bottle of water on the coffee table. Are you hot?*"

"*But what if she has to wee?*" *interrupted Samuel, to take the attention off David who was radiating guilt like a thief caught red-handed.*

"*What were you two talking about while I was downstairs?*" *asked Julie, noticing her friends' strange behaviour.*

"Films," the two boys lied in unison. "And then we wondered if you hadn't fallen asleep next to Auntie!" added Samuel.

"Well I didn't, as you can see. All right, well, let's go. And stop freaking out. If Auntie wakes up, she'll drink. And if she drinks, she'll go right back to sleep."

"How do you know for sure?"

"Because I just spent five minutes dissolving two sleeping pills in her water bottle! That's why it took me so long. Now you know! So, are we going or not?"

The two boys looked at one another to be sure they'd heard right. Upon seeing the other's expression, they realized they had. They mumbled incomprehensibly, then realized they were alone in the room. Julie had already disappeared through the window.

The Twisted Wood snack bar and arcade was a good fifteen-minute walk away. To get there, they had to walk along Mouettes Beach, then turn left towards the dunes, and finally cross through a tiny part of the Pays de Monts forest, which was bordered by Avenue de la Pège. The place was well-known among tourists and was located near several campsites. In fact, it wasn't really called the Twisted Wood at all—that was the name of the closest campsite, which was just a few metres up the road. But local youths must have found the name poetic enough to adopt it for the arcade as well. And the name had stuck, known to all as the place with the twinkling, multicoloured lights, where the sounds of arcade games accompanied the kaleidoscopic emotions of childhood summers.

"Did you really spike Auntie's water?" asked Samuel as he took the lead in his self-appointed role as scout. David didn't mind—he was happy to follow along behind, beside Julie.

"It's not a big deal," she said calmly. "If she hasn't drunk it by the time we get home, I'll empty it out and put in new water."

David didn't know what to think. He had been so excited at the idea of the magical time they would have after sneaking out to the arcade, but since leaving, he'd had a strange feeling. He had turned around discreetly several times to make sure no one was following them. He couldn't explain it, or even describe the sensation, but he felt ill at ease. *Maybe he was just worried about getting caught. After all, if they ran into any of his stepfather's or Fabien's colleagues, they were toast. And the moon was nearly full. He had tried to forget about the legend of the hanged woman, but it kept coming back, like the incessant waves at the beach.* Calm down, stupid, you're just scared, *he told himself, thinking of how his friends would tease him if he spoke up.*

The three children turned away from the waves, towards the dunes. The sea was calm. The loud daytime crashing of water on sand had quietened to a gentle melody. The shadows of maritime pines drew nearer.

"This way," said Samuel, pointing to the path through the woods. "We're almost there."

Their feet finally left the tiring sand and were met with firm earth covered in a thin layer of pine needles. The vegetation quickly grew so dense that they could hardly see. The trees surrounded them claustrophobically and occasionally erased the path altogether. The children stayed close together, shoulder to shoulder. The darkness enveloped them and a putrid stench—the nauseating smell of seaweed blended with that of damp wood—travelled up from the sea whispering "Emilie".

"Do you believe in werewolves?" Julie asked suddenly, breaking the silence that had settled over them since they had entered the forest.

"What? Of course not," replied Samuel, pulling an incredulous face.

"What about vampires?" Julie insisted.

"Nope."

"And the living dead?" she continued, watching her friends squirm in reaction to the images she savvily conjured up in their imaginations.

"Like in the Michael Jackson video?" asked David.

"Yeah," she replied. "They were real, apparently."

"Yeah right," said Samuel with a nervous laugh. "We're men, not boys. I don't believe in any of that. My brother says the real monsters in this world are men. And he's right. A zombie has nothing on my brother when he's angry or drunk."

"What about you, David?" Julie persisted, curious.

"I . . . I don't know . . ."

"He believes that the hanged woman haunts the living on the night of the full moon," Samuel interrupted. "But his real monster is his stepfather. A bloody vicious alcoholic. And he's nothing next to Red. That guy's scarier than all of Michael's zombies put together!"

Julie's face instantly fell, but the boys were too busy scanning the darkness with their torches to notice. She could hardly believe what she'd just heard. She suddenly felt like she was in danger, realizing all at once that they were just children walking through a strange forest in the middle of the night.

"What does he mean, David?" she asked, her voice thick with worry. "What's this about your stepfather? And a hanged woman? And Red?"

"It's nothing," replied the boy. "Just silly nonsense."

The children were overjoyed when the path finally led them to a paved road, down which other kids their age (some of them alone, others with their parents) were walking determinedly. They were all headed in the same direction, like insects attracted by artificial light. Julie was relieved to see so many people.

"And here we are!" said Samuel, raising his arms in a messianic gesture.

Just across from them, bright lanterns lit up the contours of a big, crowded building. When he saw all of the screens, David realized that the new games had arrived. He hurried to join Samuel who was already on his way to the till to buy tokens. He pulled Julie along after him.

"Wow! I feel like we've just landed on another planet! This is nothing like my afternoons at the beach with Auntie!" she exclaimed.

"Yeah, there are so many people!" replied David ecstatically.

The speakers at the adjacent snack bar blasted out "Holiday Rap", the latest hit, and the smell of candyfloss wafted through the entire building.

"Hey, factory kids, back again this year?"

David immediately recognized the teen sitting behind the till. It was Olivier, who had been working the same holiday job since their first summer in Saint-Hilaire. They ran into him every year.

"Hi, Olivier! How are you?" asked David.

"I'm great, guys, thanks! Glad to see you!"

For the boys, Olivier was the exact opposite of the young men in their hometown. With his blue eyes and constant smile, he'd been kind and welcoming to them when they had first turned up with David's mother. Exploring the arcade for the first time that evening, the boys hadn't even tried to hide their awe at all of the new games—back home there was only the dusty old Pac-Man at the local café. Since it was a quiet night (the rain didn't help), Olivier had left his post to explain how the different games worked. He even took a few tokens from the till to give them demonstrations and win them a few credits as they looked on in admiration.

"Look here. This is Time Pilot. We got it just last week. It's a shoot'em-up. This one is Spy Hunter, you'll love it . . . Ah, and this is my favourite, though one of the hardest: Dragon's Lair. Pure genius! And over there . . ."

He had gone on like that the whole night. And ever since, David and Samuel had always looked forward to seeing Olivier. Fabien said he was a poof (a term his little brother didn't really understand), but the boys thought he was incredibly cool.

"Ah," said Olivier, surprised to see the blonde girl standing just behind them. "A new recruit?"

"This is Julie," explained Samuel. "A siren we caught in our nets!" he added, elbowing David as he spoke. "It's her first summer here, and her first time at the Twisted Wood."

"Pleased to meet you, Miss Julie! I hope you'll like it here. And if these two rascals start banging too hard on the machines, you come tell me, all right?"

"Okay," Julie replied shyly.

"So, here you are: thirty francs in tokens! Plus a few extra on the house. Have fun!"

The three friends hurried over to the games and spent their evening moving from one to another. The moon took full possession of the sky outside as the hours ticked past hurriedly, as if frightened by the monsters the children had now forgotten. Much to the boys' surprise, Julie had a great time—not just watching, but also playing. They both went strangely silent when she beat their record at Donkey Kong. Samuel insisted she must have played it before, that there was no other way. But Julie swore on Auntie's life (at that exact moment, the old woman, only half awake, reached out and took a drink from her water bottle) that it was the very first time she had ever been to an arcade. David burst out laughing when he saw his friend's face. Samuel was so disgusted to have lost that he put in a new token, and then a few more, to defend his honour—all in vain.

They took turns playing all of the different games ("Hey, it's just not my night," Samuel admitted as he gave up on the gorilla with a smile) before returning to the till to change out what money they had left.

Around one o'clock in the morning, as the arcade lights turned off one by one, Julie lost their last token in a bitter boss fight and said it was time to go. Their eyes red from concentrating on the pixels, the tired children started home. They walked hurriedly through the forest, then slowed down again upon reaching the beach.

"That was fantastic!" exclaimed Julie with her arms around her friends' shoulders. "Thanks to you, I've had an amazing holiday!"

"I think you have to jump and shoot fireballs at the same time," mumbled Samuel, reliving the last game.

He spent the entire walk replaying a level he promised himself he would win the next time. He was so engrossed in his thoughts that he didn't realize how far ahead of his friends he was. Julie and David watched him go, enjoying his mumbled suggestions.

"He's a funny one," said Julie.

"Yep," replied David. "And you haven't even seen him at his best!"

"Do you think she'll come home?"

"Who?"

"That girl, Emilie. I can't stop thinking about her."

"I don't know. But I hope so. People don't just disappear," David

reassured her. "I'm sure we'll see her at the beach with her family tomorrow."

They clung to this idea, repeating it silently in their heads like a mantra, like an incantation designed to scare away a mysterious monster whose features neither of them could describe.

"I have something for you," Julie said, coming to a sudden stop.

David, who thought he must have misheard, turned around, an inquisitive look on his face. Behind her, the waves lapped gently at the shore, as though they had quietened in anticipation of the scene which was about to unfold.

"What?"

"Are you deaf?" she teased. "I have something for you."

"For me? Uh . . . What is it?" he asked awkwardly.

Julie rifled through her shorts pocket and pulled out what David at first thought was a piece of string.

"It's a friendship bracelet. Do you know what that is?"

"No . . . I mean, I've seen them before," he lied to seem cool.

"You give them to people you care about. When you put it on, you have to make a wish. And when all the threads break, the wish will come true. I got it from a vending machine near the girls' toilets. I thought it would be nice to give you one. I got one for me, too. Here, I'll help you put it on. Left or right?"

"Uh . . . right."

David watched as Julie came closer and took his wrist. He remembered the face that had appeared to him a few days earlier when he'd tried to fall asleep alone in his bed, ignoring the adults in the next room. It had seemed so beautiful and soothing to him then, that he had clung to it all night. And now, on Mouettes Beach, in the light of the moon, he saw that same face again, but it was so close to him this time that he could feel her skin on his and hear her breath.

"Now me. Right arm, please," she said cheerfully.

He took her hand.

"No, my right, not yours, silly!" she laughed. "Now, let's close our eyes and make a wish."

A few seconds later, when David reopened his eyes, Julie was already staring at him. He felt like she was closer to him than she had been just before. She seemed to be waiting for something, but he wasn't sure what. A strange silence came over them. Even the waves seemed frozen to the spot. Maybe spontaneous freezing exists, like spontaneous combustion, *he thought as he felt a chill in the bottom half of his face.*

Just then, several words shouted through the darkness broke the silence and interrupted the moment. Julie and David turned their heads at exactly the same time in a move worthy of the "Thriller" dance, looking for the source of the sound. The noise of the waves, the nocturnal animals, and the branches bending in the breeze seemed to return to their usual volume. They finally worked out where the sound had come from when it echoed again through the night. They glanced at each other one last time, then moved on, both promising to relive the experience as soon as possible. They started running and giggling as they made their way towards Samuel, who was sitting on the sand a few metres away, shouting at the sea. "Laugh all you want! But I'm sure she's played Donkey Kong before! She must have!"

Around one thirty, Olivier closed the till and locked the door to the storeroom.

He walked around the arcade, picking up fizzy drink cans that uncoordinated or simply inconsiderate kids had left lying just next to the bin. He checked all of the exits for the last time. Then he pulled down the metal hatch and left the building behind, making his way towards the car park. He had bought his old Peugeot 104 with his earnings from the previous summer. It was rusty and pretty banged up on one side. And the passenger-side window didn't close properly, which was a pain in the winter. But Olivier loved the car despite all of this. It was his first, and he had bought it with his own money.

As he was fumbling for his keys in the back pocket of his jeans, out of the corner of his eye he noticed a movement over to his left. He turned his head and waited a few seconds to see if the person hiding behind a parked car would come out. But nothing happened.

Olivier began doubting what he thought he'd seen. He was tired, and the neon lights and loud music in the arcade could frazzle your senses. He inserted his key into the lock but noticed the movement again. He was sure of it this time. Someone was hiding. He could have sworn he'd seen the shadow move towards another car. He quickly got into the 104, turned the key in the ignition and put the car in reverse. He didn't know if the person was after him, but he didn't want to investigate any further. Maybe just kids messing around. Or maybe . . .

He couldn't resist the urge to look up at the moon.

Not full yet.

Soon.

It couldn't be her.

He kicked himself for even thinking about the legend. He was too old to believe he could run into a woman who had been dead for years. All those kids who came and spent their pocket money at the arcade could believe it, but not him. He was the guy who handed out the tokens and owned his first car . . . He wasn't a child any longer.

Nevertheless, Olivier took one last look in the rear-view mirror. Nothing. He accelerated a bit too quickly (he imagined stalling or, worse still, flooding the engine like in all those stupid horror films), but managed to leave the car park and put some distance between himself and his childish fears.

That was one of the last nights he was ever seen at the Twisted Wood.

August 1986

Paul Vermont had received another letter. More virulent this time. More aggressive. More real.

He paced the factory with the letter safely hidden in the inside pocket of his tweed jacket. His employees hardly dared look at him. Many of them were already on holiday in Saint-Hilaire; enjoying their comfortable bungalows and plotting against him. Maybe they were just threats. Empty promises made by angry fathers needing to feed their families, who would remember that Paul Vermont was a good, honest man when it came down to it. Some of them would remember how his wife served cocktails at the parties they hosted in the garden of their summer house, even as she fought her illness. *Are men born mad, or do they become so with the passage of time and accumulated hardships?* he wondered.

Paul stepped into his office and closed the door. He didn't know who was responsible for the leak but somehow people knew about the factory's situation. The letters were arriving more often, and the threats were intensifying. The press was involved now too. A short article had appeared in the local newspaper—just a few laconic lines, but they had been enough to feed the rumours. And to motivate people to write these anonymous letters. Most of the letters expressed vague warnings without any real danger ("You're ruining your father's legacy", "Do you sleep better at night knowing you've reduced dozens of families to poverty?", "Instead of offering us cocktails and barbecues, you should have given us ropes to hang ourselves like your wife . . ."), but the one he'd received this morning was different. He was terrified. Would he have to renege on his promise? Would the danger in these lines force him to back out of a pact which he would never again be in a position to honour due to the factory's financial situation? Could he live with the weight on his shoulders—a weight much heavier than the fate of his employees?

Paul sat down at his desk and dialled the extension for the welding workshop.

"Yes?" said a gruff voice.

"Could you please ask Franck to come to my office?"

"Just as soon as I find him," replied the workshop manager before hanging up without another word.

A few minutes later, Franck came into the office and stood in front of the director's desk. "Sir?"

"I got a letter this morning. Another one. But this one deserves our attention," explained Paul as he pulled it from his pocket and handed it to Red.

The man read it, then gave it back.

"How did they find out?" Paul asked.

"I don't know. Sometimes people remember."

"I was so discreet, though," said Paul, speaking mostly to himself.

"I'm heading to Les Mouettes in a few days," said Franck, knowing his boss would understand what he was implying.

"Franck, I made a promise. A promise I cannot break. You're the only person in this whole bloody factory who understands me. And you made me a promise in return."

"I know."

"And, despite this letter, I can't bring myself to go back on my word. Do you understand?"

"Yes, sir."

"So, while you're there, make sure we both remain men of our word, will you?"

"A promise is a promise," said Red gravely.

In rural regions like this one, a simple exchange of words was enough to seal a pact as ironclad as any contract. It held more conviction and honour than any official document.

"What if things go wrong?" asked Franck, his eyes glued to the man across from him.

"I have total and utter faith in you. You'll know how to solve the problem and avoid any danger."

"Very well, sir."

"Franck?"

"Yes?"

"Thank you. Thank you for everything. Men of honour are rare these days. You're the only one I know."

"It will all be okay, Mr Vermont. You can count on me. I'll make sure of it, day and night. A promise is a promise."

Chapter 9
Thursday

The next morning, the three children went their separate ways after enjoying a copious breakfast Auntie had prepared. David and Samuel didn't say a single thing beyond the usual pleasantries, so worried were they that the old woman was about to tell them off for drugging her. But the scolding never came. Auntie simply said she was more tired than usual and decided to rest in her room for an hour before joining them at the beach with Julie. "We'll see you there, boys. Be good in the meantime!" Julie and her friends watched as the old woman lethargically closed the door. A loud snoring resonated from her bedroom just a few seconds later.

"Let's go!" said Samuel, eager to put some distance between himself and Auntie.

"All right," agreed David. "See you later?" he asked, turning to Julie.

"Of course! You won't get rid of me that easily!" she replied.

As soon as she'd spoken, however, an unusual glint appeared in her eyes. Sadness emanated not only from her gaze but from her entire body; it was apparent in her gestures and in the silence that followed her words. The same ferocious sadness took hold of David and Samuel, who understood at that moment that their friendship had an expiration date and that it was terribly near. They all realized they only had two days left together. On Saturday, Julie would leave them, and the two boys would return to their tower block, far from the waves, the sun, and the smiles.

"I even miss this stupid place when we're back home!" David admitted as they walked past the big abandoned house a few minutes later.

As if he'd guessed his best friend's thoughts, Samuel suggested they finish their holiday with a bang. "We could do it tomorrow, our last night together," he said.

"Do what?"

"What we promised to do last year. You didn't really think I'd forgotten, did you?"

"Visit the hanged woman's house?"

"Yes!" Samuel replied enthusiastically. "We can tell our parents we're sleeping over at Julie's this time. They'll want to take advantage of their last night, too. They don't really care what we do. I bet they'll be happy not to have to look after us!"

"Do you think Julie will be up for it?"

"That girl isn't afraid of anything. I'm sure she'll say yes. I mean, if you're there, she'll definitely agree. We'll ask her tomorrow. It'll be a surprise."

The boys caught sight of a police car as they turned towards the beach. The car slowed as it passed them, then continued patrolling down the road.

"They still haven't found her," mumbled David as he turned his head to follow the police car. The thought darkened his already sullen mood.

Julie. Emilie.

The two girls would disappear from his life the moment he got in the back of his stepfather's Renault 5. He didn't even know the latter, but he still felt a kind of affection for her. He was sure she would have been a great friend for Julie. They would have got on perfectly. And David couldn't help but smile when he thought that if all four of them had run off to the arcade together, Olivier would have thought they were twin sisters since they looked so much alike.

The day went by in a flash. A radiant but threatening blur that quickly devoured the hours, which the children wished would last forever. The three friends joked about their adventures the night before, going back over each game, each victory and loss. Samuel noticed the bracelets tied to his friends' wrists. He smiled and began coming up with excuses to leave them alone together for a few minutes.

"I'm going to piss in the ocean. Don't follow me or you might get radiation poisoning!", "Stay put, it's my turn to get the ice cream", and even, "I'm going to see Auntie, I'm sure she's dying to talk to me but doesn't dare! She's very shy, like you, David!"

That evening, a full moon rose slowly over the sea. It looked as though it had only just escaped from the tumultuous waters, exiting the waves after a long dive among the souls of the decomposing pirates whispering secrets which could only be heard once the sun had set.

The children went home, tired from their exploits the night before.

David kissed his mother. He was afraid she might ask him questions, certain that she somehow knew he hadn't really slept over at Samuel's. But it didn't happen. She hugged him especially tight, like the day when he'd left for summer camp for the first time and she hadn't been able to hold back her tears in front of the impatient bus driver and camp counsellors.

"What is it, Mum?" he asked worriedly.

"Nothing, sweetheart," she replied. "I just haven't seen you since last night. That's all."

"Why haven't you guys come to the beach this year?"

"We have some things we need to take care of. That's why. You know, things are going to be difficult soon. Work . . . We may never go back to the factory. We probably won't come back here next summer . . ."

"Why? Why not?" stammered David, feeling tears prick his eyelids.

"They're grown-up problems, sweetheart. But don't worry, we'll find jobs elsewhere."

"I . . . I don't want to go anywhere else. I want to come back here with Samuel and Julie."

"We'll find a solution, I promise. In the meantime, there's something I want you to do. We won't be here tonight. There's a meeting, you know, like the one from the other day. And children can't come. You'll stay here for a cosy night in. I've rented you a film and made your dinner. We won't be back too late. But please, whatever you do, don't leave the bungalow. Okay?"

"Why can't I come with you, Mum?"

"Because it's a full moon tonight, love. And sometimes bad things happen during a full moon . . ."

Two hours later, after his shower and a good long cry in the bathroom, David watched as the adults left in silence, their faces drawn. As the darkness approached, he decided to turn on all the lights.

He didn't understand anything his mother had told him. He thought back to what his stepfather had said in the kitchen: "Your mother's crazy."

Could it be true? Were her strange words proof of her madness? Why had his mother been acting so oddly since that night when she had seemed possessed by the sombre melancholy of the big house she had been staring at through the window? Why did David feel like part of his world was about to cave in on this particularly bright night? He felt an urge to run to Samuel's, to let his best friend comfort him, before going to Julie's and watching the film his mother had rented with her and Auntie, all four of them keeping each other company. He also hoped that the wish he had made in secret when Julie had given him the friendship bracelet would come true.

He wanted Emilie to join them.

He wanted her to come back safe and sound.

4

This is it, I thought. I could feel the fear in the pit of my stomach.

That ill-fated night during the summer of 1986.

The night when the full moon shone for the last time over a house haunted by people's madness.

I can still see them. Drunk and impulsive. As crazy and agitated as pirates who had decided to burn their patron goddess.

One more chapter. One more night with Julie, even though we didn't speak. We were like bottles tossed about by the tides, trying desperately to deliver the messages we guarded in our hearts. We were certain that once the storm had passed, we would find each other again and go for a walk along Mouettes Beach, just like we had the night before on our way home from the arcade.

But they decided otherwise.

There was no last smile.

No nocturnal visit to the big house.

Madness alone lit up the night.

Chapter 10

David woke up. He didn't remember falling asleep.

He lay still on the sofa for a while longer, gradually letting his senses adjust to reality. The glaring light from the ceiling fixture accentuated the silence in the house.

Oh right, I'm all alone, *he remembered.*

He sat up, stretched, yawned loudly and at length—a sure sign that he could do with more sleep—and stiffly made his way to the kitchen. He opened the cupboard, grabbed a glass, and filled it from the tap. His mother's words continued to dance through his mind. He couldn't wrap his head around it. Never come back here? Never walk down Avenue des Mouettes again? Never see Julie again when he'd already imagined their reunion the following year? She would be lying on her towel next to Auntie, in the same spot where he had seen her for the very first time. Her blonde hair would be just as radiant and her features just as fine and flawless as on the morning she'd first waved to him. To make sure he knew she was still the same, that nothing had changed, she would say something like: "That wasn't very nice to make me miss you all year . . ." Then he'd say hello to Auntie and give her a big hug, and they'd tell each other everything they hadn't been able to fit into the many letters they would have exchanged in the months they'd been apart. The sun would be shining. Samuel would arrive and they would all laugh again. And Emilie would be there, too, just a few metres away, with her parents.

He noticed something strange as he brought his drink to his lips.

Fireflies, *he thought at first. David watched as the bright dots danced through the air outside. But when he looked closer, he realized that they couldn't be insects: their irregular movements stopped too abruptly, and their phosphorescence was an unusual shade of orangey-red. David glued his face to the window pane. The sound of glass shattering on the ground reverberated through the air, though the boy didn't pay it any attention. His empty hand curled into a fist, expressing the anger that his mouth, silent and agape, could not utter.*

He could see now, through the large garden, that the boss's house was on fire. Tall flames writhed as they worked their way skyward. Their chaotic shadows danced against the silhouettes of onlookers gathered in sparse groups. He was sure that they were smiling at the dramatic show before them. It was like a bad dream. David closed his eyes tightly, hoping to escape from this scene which—he thought, hoped, pleaded—was a product of his imagination. But when he opened them again, the flames were still there. The fire licked gleefully at the wooden façade, spewing dark, cloying smoke as it reached higher still to devour the gabled windows set into the roof. The spectators' reddened faces looked like demonic masks. They were still and watchful, like the curious folk who had patiently waited at the gallows for young women to be declared guilty of witchcraft centuries before.

A tiny piece of glowing wood fell against the window, millimetres from David's face. He finally realized that what he had taken for fireflies were actually tiny pieces of the big house, spectral lights dotting the night trying to convey one last message; stars dying under the flat, expressionless light of the full moon.

He didn't notice the tears streaming down his face.

He forgot about his mother's instructions.

David ran to the door and out into the night.

It was around quarter past midnight when Pierre Mathieu, the firefighter on call at Saint-Hilaire-de-Riez, got the call. He immediately flipped on the siren to alert his nephews, Sébastien and Bruno, hoping that they were in bed at home and not hitting on tourists in a bar somewhere. Five minutes later, the two young men were standing before him in their uniforms. They looked a little sleepy but fit to serve. It's a miracle, *thought Pierre with a sigh.*

The three men hurried to the fire engine, turned on the flashing lights, and sped to the address they'd been given on the Avenue des Mouettes. When they got there, the house was already lost. Which was surprising. The person who had called had described the fire as burning along just one side of the house. Now, the entire structure was engulfed in flames. Fires didn't generally spread that fast. Unless . . .

Pierre ordered one of his nephews to unravel the hose and hook it up to the fire hydrant. Sébastien fought his innate clumsiness, doing his best to remember the exercises he had performed not nearly enough times, but he managed despite it all. Pierre waited nervously, hose in hand, for the water pressure to surge. Back-up will be here soon from the other fire departments, *he thought to himself as he walked towards the building.* Police, too. All I have to do is contain the fire and keep it from spreading. *Meanwhile, Bruno was on a quest for information. He got a few answers from the onlookers (No, no one was inside. Yes, the fire had intensified rapidly. "I always wanted to be a firefighter. Does it work on the ladies?" Gas? "No, no one has lived here for years." "Did you know this house is haunted?"), before ordering everybody back past the perimeter so that the professionals could do their work.*

As he returned to his uncle's side, he glanced towards the beach and noticed a second column of smoke. It was much smaller (he imagined it was likely an unauthorized barbecue hosted by pretty Swedish tourists), but he let Pierre know anyway.

"Where?" shouted his uncle.

"Over there, on Mouettes Beach."

"If it's on the sand, there's no risk it'll spread. We'll see what we can do when back-up shows up. For now, let's handle this bastard!"

Bruno stood by Pierre's side and watched as the stream of water arched overhead and crashed down into the hanged woman's house. Everyone in the area knew the legend that had grown out of her suicide. The pirates, the whispers, the madness . . . Just a harmless story, *he thought.* So why go after her? Why try to kill a ghost?

Chapter 11

Red didn't move.

He watched the house burn. He listened as the beams groaned in pain. He looked on as the windows shattered one after the other from the extreme heat.

As if to echo his inner suffering, his scar came to life and burned his cheek.

Hold my hand.

No, you're big now.

He chased the words from his mind, turned away from the fire, and made his way towards the beach.

"A promise is a promise," he mumbled.

A strange feeling came over Samuel when he realized something unusual was going on. He didn't know why—maybe because his brother had seemed particularly agitated for several days now, or because he had made him promise not to leave the bungalow all night—but he was sure that the feeling had to do with the commotion outside. He thought of David and Julie. Had they heard the sirens, too? He decided to disobey Fabien and leave the house to find out where the shadowy figures he saw passing his window were all going.

Sitting behind the till at the arcade, Olivier watched as a column of smoke rose up into the sky. Forest fires weren't a rare occurrence at this time of year, but he was certain this was something else. The fire seemed to be in town. The billowing black mass slowly blocked his view of the full moon. He thought of the girl the police had been looking for over the past few days. One of them had even come to *question him, clearly hoping for answers. ("Do you recognize her? Have you seen her? Are you sure?") But he hadn't seen her. And when the police officer thanked him and said goodbye, staring at him a beat too long, Olivier had felt guilty. For what, he didn't know, but he had looked down to rid himself of his uneasiness, pretending to count the tokens piled up in front of him.*

Julie heard a muffled sound from outside. She got out of bed and stuck her head out of her bedroom window. A siren blared. She made her way to the lounge, where Auntie was snoring loudly, in a deep, artificially induced sleep. Julie considered waking her but decided against it. She would go out alone to find out what was going on and why the neighbours were standing in the alleyway staring at something she couldn't see from her room.

David walked around the side of the bungalow and past the conifer hedge, then made his way through the compact crowd that surrounded the big house. Nearly fifty people watched as the three firefighters battled the flames. The water shot out of the firehose, climbing up through the air before slamming into the inexplicable inferno. A side wall collapsed and the onlookers took several paces back as the entryway where Mrs Vermont had ended her life was revealed. Driven by curiosity, the crowd then inched closer again, craning their necks to see a bit more, ignoring the shouted warnings from the young firefighter. They seemed to be hoping that they would catch a glimpse of the skeleton of the woman who used to serve them cocktails in the verdant garden they were now trampling, as though she might still be swinging from the beam.

David was crying.

The air, which was thick with unbearable smells, and the smoke, which whirled around like a kite caught in a storm, were burning his eyes.

But his tears also came from somewhere deeper within. The absurd idea that the destruction of this house would mean not only the end of his holiday, but the end of his innocence and his childhood stubbornly refused to leave his mind. Tormented by the scene and by

*his mother's strangely prophetic words, he believed that the fate of
the house was tied not only to his own (*if the house is saved, we'll
be able to come back next year*) but also to Julie's (*if the house
is saved, I'll see her again and listen closely to everything she
says*) and to Emilie's. And even though his final thought (*if the
house is saved, Emilie will be too*) seemed morbid and strange to
him, he clung to it with all his strength, clutching it in his balled
fists, giving himself over to it like a superstitious sailor abandons
his fate to a goddess of the sea.*

*The fire roared, growing more intense. The flames climbed higher,
reaching for the impassive moon, doing their best to brand their
presence onto the memories of those watching for years to come. An
ominous creak rang out over the crackling of the burning wood. A
satisfied "ooh!" escaped from the crowd as the onlookers realized
the finale was near. "No!" David couldn't help but exclaim when
it became clear to him that the roof was about to cave in.*

*Just as some spectators were beginning to express their impatience
("this can't go on all night") and others were making bets on the
exact time when the building would collapse, a second firehose,
attached to another fire engine which had just arrived, sprang into
action and delayed the crowd's moment of gratification.*

A battle between the two elements ensued.

The roof wavered but remained in place.

*As the flames receded, the firefighters moved closer, slowly and
respectfully, step by step, as if treading on hallowed ground.*

*The police ordered the crowd back, doing nothing to quell the
general frustration.*

David did as he was told, but kept his eyes glued to the house.

"Maybe she managed to get out," said a voice.

*Samuel appeared, placing his hand on his best friend's shoulder.
Tears had left vertical furrows down his cheeks, and David noticed
that his own face was also covered in a thin layer of ash.*

*"Why?" he asked without tearing his gaze from the flames, which
now seemed to be huddling over in fear.*

*"I don't know . . . She didn't deserve this . . . The hanged woman
didn't deserve this."*

"No," agreed David, comforted by his friend's presence. "But it's a full moon. Maybe she got out in time."

The two boys stood there in the night for a while, hoping that the ghost—whom they feared and whose very existence they refuted in the daytime—had escaped. They tried to remember Mrs Vermont, to honour her memory. They were saddened as they imagined the pirates writhing in pain on the ocean floor behind them.

Slowly but surely, the opaque veil that had filled the sky for hours began to dissipate. The moon shone through the remaining smoke, reclaiming ownership of the shadows.

"Look, over there," Samuel said, pointing. "They're all here."

And they were. His mother, his stepfather, and the other employees David had seen at the bungalow that first evening. Red was the only one missing. They all observed the destruction in silence. He could see discreet smiles on the men's faces. Slight smirks that spoke volumes. The children watched as the police approached and the small group dispersed. The officers were questioning everyone present, noting down their doubt or certainty on the subject before moving on to the next person.

"I have to get home," said David, his eyes still on his mother.

She hadn't even noticed him. She was studying the ground at her feet.

"Me, too," replied Samuel. "If my brother catches me out here, he'll kill me! See you tomorrow!" He disappeared, breaking into a jog as he rounded the corner.

The firefighters—there were eight now by David's count—kept hosing the building.

Pierre and his nephews kept up the fight.

As if weary of their silly game, the flames suddenly stopped their hypnotic dance. Thick, black smoke rose one last time into the sky, then dispersed in the sea breeze, like the final breath of a dying animal.

The crowd admitted defeat, casting a final glance at the beast who'd died too soon. The onlookers then regretfully disbanded, disappointed to be so abruptly deprived of entertainment.

The firefighters took a break and exchanged information with the police.

This wasn't the first time they had worked together. Pierre even knew the newest recruit to the force, a young man from Saint-Hilaire who had run wild with his nephews before finding his calling.

"Hello, Henri."

"Hi, Pierre. You guys did well. The fire could have spread to the surrounding houses," noted the young officer.

"Thank you. Luckily the second team got here quickly. Otherwise . . ."

"What do you think?" asked Henri, lifting his chin towards the ruins where three firefighters were sifting through the debris on the hunt for any remaining flames.

"Arson. No doubt about it," replied Pierre.

"How can you be so sure?"

"Usually fires have one point of origin, and they spread from there. You can trace their paths by taking the terrain, the wind, and construction materials into account. No one has lived in this house for years, so it wasn't an accidental kitchen fire, for example. When we got here, I immediately noticed there were several points of origin. I counted at least three. And the flames started outside."

"Kids?"

"Teenagers, adults . . . what does it matter? Whoever it was wanted to burn this bloody house to the ground. That's for sure."

"All right, thank you."

"Henri!" added Pierre as the police officer started to walk away.

"Yes?"

"When we got here, there was another smaller fire, over there, on Mouettes Beach. We didn't focus on it because we had too much to handle here. Plus, on the sand . . ."

"Okay, I'll go and check it out," replied Henri. "If I don't see you again tonight, tell Josie hello from me. I'll try to drop in for coffee sometime soon."

"Sounds good. We're going to let the second team finish up here. I need a cold shower."

"See you soon!"

"Oh, hey, Henri?"

"Yes?"

"No trouble with my nephews? No funny business recently? Even speeding tickets?"

"What nephews?" replied the officer with a smile. *"Enjoy your shower, Pierre!"*

As he walked down Avenue des Mouettes, Henri Bichaut thought back to his teenage years spent with Sébastien and Bruno. Nights at the beach, girls, pot . . . Good thing old Pierre doesn't know the half of it! *he thought with a wry smile as he reached the beach.*

Less than ten minutes later (once he'd stopped vomiting, crying and shaking), Henri ran back the way he had come. He shouted to alert his boss who worriedly watched as his youngest officer drew closer, his face as white and terrified as a child who'd seen a ghost.

"Christ! What's going on?" shouted the sergeant, annoyed at Henri's lack of professionalism.

"I . . . I . . . On the beach . . . It's . . ."

"Get a hold of yourself! What's happened?"

"On the beach . . . The fire . . ."

"Snap out of it, Henri! What the bloody hell is on the beach?"

"I think . . . I think it's . . . Emilie."

Chapter 12

The Deaf Man

But she was of the world, which fairest things exposes
To fates the most forlorn;
A rose, she too hath lived as long as live the roses,
The space of one brief morn.

PART TWO

Whispers from the earth

"Do you believe in ghosts?"

"Ghosts? No . . . No, I don't—"

"You should. This is all really one big ghost story. About the dead who come back to life . . . And about the living who are already dead . . . They're all ghosts. And they all have a message to share. Ponder that. Never forget it. Repeat it to yourself and keep it in mind before your memories become ghosts as well . . ."

August 1986

The day after the fire, the police asked Emilie's parents to come down to the station in Saint-Hilaire-de-Riez. They were hesitant as they stepped inside, both intrigued and frightened by what they might learn. The person they had spoken to on the phone had been rather evasive, mentioning only new evidence found during the night, without any further details.

Henri welcomed them in. Like them, he looked like he hadn't slept in days. He offered them a drink, then sat them down in a small room to wait for his boss, who was expected any minute. Less than five minutes later, the sergeant came into the room holding an opaque plastic bag. He sat down across from them. Henri remained standing, his back against the far wall.

"Thank you for coming in so quickly, Mr and Mrs Dupuis," began the sergeant.

"What's going on?" the mother asked impatiently.

"It may not be much, but we have some new evidence," he explained.

"Have you found her? Have you found our little girl?" implored Mr Dupuis.

"I can't answer that question just yet. First, I need to show you something."

The sergeant put the bag on the table and pulled out its contents, slowly, respectfully.

Emilie's parents remained silent. With fear in their eyes, they stared at the blue shorts, pink T-shirt, and the pair of sandals placed before them.

This is it, thought Henri as he watched. *Any minute now they'll fall to pieces. They'll shout, cry, demand an explanation.*

I'll have to explain that these clothes were found next to the corpse. Then I'll describe their daughter's badly burned body. Their only child, huddled in the foetus position, her ankles and wrists bound with wire. I won't mention how hot the fire must have been due to the petrol. Or the way skin blisters and cracks, then disappears altogether. Or how human fat melts, fuelling the fire. Or how quickly hair ignites. Or the way eyes dry up and pop. I won't tell them that the face they loved to kiss no longer exists. I'll forget to mention the smell of charred meat I spent the entire night trying to clean off my body in the shower. I won't show them the photographs we took before moving the body. They would see nothing but a revolting, blackened corpse, and the image would forever tinge their memories of their daughter. Here come the first tears. She's leaning into his arms. He embraces her, it's a reflex, unthinking, drained by exhaustion. Their own deaths have never been so imminent. They must feel it, too. Few parents would survive such a . . .

The sergeant gave them a few minutes before speaking. He had never had to handle a case like this before. Despite his rank, he didn't know any more about kidnappings and murders than the young Henri. Saint-Hilaire was a small seaside town. Speeding. Drunk driving. A break-in or two, especially during the summer when holidaymakers spent carefree afternoons lounging at the beach. But a kidnapping and murder . . .

Never.

What he wanted, above all else, was to flee this room and its tragedy, which seemed to be smothering him, depriving him of oxygen. He wanted to get back to the routine of his small town, usually as regular as clockwork. He decided the first thing he would do once the parents had left was take down the missing person flyers. A symbolic gesture to help him move on and forget he had ever seen the girl's charcoal-black skeleton. He would probably sit down on the beach to toss his memories of the night into the sea. The only way to keep from drowning was to dive into the arms of the living. He would go home, take his wife and daughter in his arms and hold them tight.

Then, the next day, he would get up and get back to managing reckless drivers and noise disturbances.

He would go back to breathing normally.

"I know this is hard for you," he finally said. "But I have to ask you a question: do you recognize these clothes?"

"I . . . When you asked what she was wearing the last time we saw her . . . We weren't sure . . . You know, girls change their clothes all the time, and . . ." sobbed Mrs Dupuis.

"I understand. Take your time. Have a good look at them and tell me when you're ready."

Henri noticed a box of tissues on a shelf. He grabbed it, noticing it had never been used, and placed it on the table.

"Thank you," mumbled Mrs Dupuis.

Those two words, uttered by a woman whose world was collapsing like a house of cards, whose only child whom she had loved more than anything had been tied up and burned, touched Henri deeply.

"Are these your daughter's clothes?" the sergeant asked gently.

He was careful not to use the past tense.

He needed an answer. To get back to his life. To get back to summer. So the couple sitting across from him could begin the long, painful process of grieving. The sergeant pleaded silently. *Say they're her shorts . . . Go back to the day you bought these sandals . . . Let your daughter go . . . Free us from her ghost . . . Don't open the door to the other possibility, which is preventing me from catching my breath . . . Don't do that . . .*

"I'm certain," the mother enunciated clearly as she dabbed at her eyes with a tissue. "These aren't Emilie's things."

The sergeant was visibly taken aback.

Henri moved away from the wall.

He knew his boss had another piece of evidence in his pocket. He knew, like the sergeant, that sometimes stress and exhaustion could compromise memory function, even though he seriously doubted that parents would not recognize clothes they had bought themselves. He watched as his boss dipped his hand into his pocket and drew out a much smaller bag.

Henri held his breath.

"I understand, madam. I believe you, but I still need to show you an object that was found near these clothes. It may be easier to recognize than a pair of shorts or a T-shirt."

When he finally showed them the contents of the bag, Emilie's father spoke up first, followed closely by his wife. "Oh, thank God," she exclaimed with a sigh of relief, joining her hands as if in prayer.

The acrid smell of smoke felt suddenly as if it were invading the minds of the two officers.

They sent the couple home, mumbling promises and reassuring platitudes. They said they would get back to them as soon as the investigation turned up anything new. Then they went back into the room and sat down at the table. Neither of them spoke for a long time. They stared at the evidence, trying to find an explanation.

But none came.

Mr Dupuis' words came back to them.

Like a ghostly whisper in the ears of the living.

Like a threatening shadow escaping from the foot of a rainbow.

"No, this isn't Emilie's either. She never wore a friendship bracelet. I'm sure of it."

Tuesday, 15th August 2017

As he did every other weekend, Henri drove his old Fiat Panda to the prison in La Roche-sur-Yon. As he travelled the thirty odd miles from Saint-Hilaire, he cursed the tourists and their leisurely pace. He was afraid he might get there too late and have to turn right back around. But luckily, a car pulled out as he arrived on Boulevard d'Angleterre, just a few metres from the entrance to the prison, buying him precious time.

1:35 p.m.

Only ten minutes until they stopped letting visitors in.

The sun shone brightly. All traces of the recent storm had disappeared, and the unbearable heat made the slightest movement uncomfortable.

He jogged through the metal door, presented his ID at reception ("Careful, Henri, you're cutting it fine!" remarked the guard, tapping his watch), filled out the form, then joined the group of visitors who were already on their way down the corridor.

The prison, much like its residents, was living on borrowed time. It had been near the top of the list of the most overpopulated prisons in France for years, but the long awaited construction of a new prison in Fontenay-le-Comte, a few miles away, was yet to materialize. The capacity there was expected to be two hundred and fifty beds, whereas La Roche only had forty.

Forty beds.

For eighty prisoners.

The visitors sat down and waited for the inmates to arrive. All of the tables in the room were taken. Women, children, parents—a hodgepodge of upended lives, loved ones who had come to top up their hope for the coming days, to tide them over until their next visit.

Less than five minutes later, a door opened. The prisoners came in and made their way towards the familiar faces as a guard closed the door behind them and went to stand against the wall. "You have forty-five minutes," he barked. The former police officer shook hands with the man who had just sat down across from him. In another place, at another time, they used to shake hands daily—at the entrance to their secondary school in Challans. That now seemed like ancient history.

"How have you been since my last visit?" asked Henri.

"All right. Keeping busy."

"Your mother sends her love. I saw her before coming here. She's got your room all ready."

"She has plenty of time. I won't be out for another six months."

"She's not feeling so well, you know."

"Is that why she doesn't come to visit any more?"

"Yes. You'll need to take good care of her when you get out. You have a lot of lost time to make up for."

"Thirty-one years to be exact."

"Yes, thirty-one years instead of forty. Your good behaviour got you nine years of freedom."

"And my innocence cost me thirty-one."

"Listen, I have a friend who owns a restaurant, and he needs help. I told him about you. He's willing to hire you for the season."

"Where?"

"Saint-Hilaire."

"Do you really think I'll ever go back there?"

"People have forgotten. It was a long time ago . . ."

"They'll never forget. For them, I'm a murderer. A child murderer. Loads of them wrote to President Mitterrand asking him to bring back the death penalty! Five years earlier, and I'd have been a goner . . ."

"There are also people who are sure you're innocent."

★

The two men silently watched the people at the other tables. Some of the prisoners were there due to sheer bad luck. A fight that went terribly wrong. A poorly prepared burglary. A clumsily handled hunting rifle. But none of them would spend thirty-one years in prison. Not one of them had been convicted of killing two young girls in the middle of summer.

"How's Nantes doing?"

"Looking good this season. That Italian coach is a miracle-worker. They've won all their practice matches."

"You know what I'm going to do when I get out of here? I'm going to see an FC Nantes game. I'll be able to blend in with the crowd and channel all my anger into football chants. We're not allowed to scream here. Not allowed to express our feelings. We keep it all inside—tears, injustice, fear. It's all locked up in here, in our own prison," explained the man, placing his index finger on his temple.

"I'll look forward to going with you," replied Henri.

When the guard gestured that their time was up, Henri promised to come back in two weeks. In the meantime, no one else would visit. His mother was too ill to come, or so Henri said. But Olivier knew the real reason she no longer visited him. He had noticed the doubt in his own mother's eyes. Then in her voice, then in her gestures, which grew increasingly distant until she no longer hugged him before leaving.

In the beginning, no one had thought him capable of such a thing.

But with time, they had all grown to believe it.

Neighbours. Friends. His own family.

Even his mother.

It took Henri over an hour to get home. During the drive, he thought back to the events of 1986. "Why do you come and visit me?" Olivier had asked back then; he had still been so young and terrified of the prison where he had just been incarcerated.

"Because I know you're innocent," the police officer had replied.

"No one believes me. My lawyer says I should plead guilty."

"Your mother believes you, and so do I. There are at least two of us, and there will be more. You have to start somewhere."

"I didn't kill them."

"I know, I know you. Don't worry, everything will be okay. Justice sometimes takes time, but it always wins out in the end."

Henri had prayed that his friend would be freed quickly. As a police officer, he knew what sort of things went on in prison. He also knew about the torture inflicted on convicts who had hurt children.

"Will you come back and see me again, Henri?" Olivier had asked, his voice pleading.

"Every two weeks. I promise."

Henri arrived home with a heavy heart. It was the same after every visit. He clung to the date in the parole decision. Nine years shaved off Olivier's sentence. He would be out in six months.

Henri opened his letterbox to find a brown manilla envelope alongside several flyers and brochures, which he immediately threw in the lobby bin. Intrigued, he turned over the envelope to see who had sent it, but there was no return address. Upon closer inspection, he realized that it must have been hand-delivered; there was no stamp or postmark. Henri climbed the stairs to his modest one-bedroom flat. A sleepy cat stretched and welcomed him by rubbing against his legs, nearly causing him to stumble.

"Jesus, Whiskas!" he grumbled, pushing the feline out of the way with his foot.

The cat meowed in displeasure, then quietly disappeared into the bedroom.

Who could have sent this? Henri wondered as he opened the envelope.

He made his way to the lounge. A few relics from his short

career as a police officer sat on the shelves of an Ikea bookcase. A diploma. A photograph of him in uniform. Nothing else. Since his resignation in 1987, he had done casual work, mostly working as a dishwasher in various seaside restaurants where the owners pretended the frozen meals they served were fresh and the tourists never complained. He was a quick learner though and had even worked for a while as a mechanic at a garage and as a mason for a local builder.

But none of the jobs were a good fit. He moved from one temp agency to another, adding meaningless lines to his CV. At the job centre, he had got to know the advisors so well that they were now on a first-name basis. His love life wasn't any more promising. He drifted from grieving widows to cheating wives. His one-night stands sometimes turned into week-long affairs, but rarely anything more.

So he was truly puzzled about who could have sent him the envelope. Henri didn't have any friends, or a girlfriend, or even an ex that might still be interested. He had no children, no siblings, no parents, nor anyone else that might write to him. At the age of fifty, this realization was a real blow. But he soldiered on. *Better to be alone than in bad company,* he would lie to himself on nights when he felt especially blue.

He pulled a dozen typewritten pages from the envelope.

The first time David saw Julie was on 12th August 1986. It was so hot that Friday that the grains of sand stuck to his skin, read the first line.

"A bloody poem!" I shouted as Samuel stepped into the house the next morning. "My final chapter is a bloody poem!"

I hadn't slept a wink.

My hands were shaking, and I was struggling to find my words. Frankly, it was a miracle I could even stand. The night before when I had read chapter twelve and finished the text, the avalanche of painful memories had brought me to tears and I had crumpled the pages in anger. I had thrown them as far as I could, railing against the twisted bastard who had dared resurrect events from my past I had thought forgotten, and made my way to the bar and the bottle of whisky.

I had spent several long hours sitting there, as sad and lonely as the sole survivor of a shipwreck on a desert island. At one point, I had stepped out onto the patio and screamed into the night air. Though I had hoped it would be powerful and liberating, the scream had turned into an indecipherable combination of sobs and words which disappeared without deafening anyone at all. The list of people who incurred my wrath that night was long. I even remembered insulting the old woman and her dog. But I had focused most of my attention on the people this retelling of my childhood had brought back into my life. Red. All the factory employees. My mother and her arsehole husband. Auntie. The police officer who had turned up early the next morning to ask questions around the neighbourhood. Samuel. Emilie.

And last but not least, Julie.

The only person I hadn't incriminated yet was myself. So I did just that during the second half of the night. I was ashamed that I had kept quiet back then, ashamed that I hadn't stood up to the adults. Ashamed that I had been so deaf, so uncomprehending, ashamed of my tears and my nightmares . . .

I went back and relived all of the scenes where I could have acted differently. I thought back to those first deaths, which I had committed myself.

All at once I was stood opposite the boss's house screaming that I no longer believed in ghost stories and pirates chanting the name of their patron goddess.

My hands, which were once again small and childlike, ripped the posters of Emilie's face from every electrical pole along Avenue des Mouettes, trying to erase the girl who had started it all.

I slit my stepfather's throat with the jagged plastic of my cereal bowl. He watched me, his eyes wide with terror, his right hand trying to staunch the blood flowing from his throat as thick bubbles of blood and oxygen swelled and then popped between his fingers, and his lips mumbled a ridiculous prayer.

I argued with my mother when she promised me everything would be okay. I shouted at her that it was a lie, that her happiness was a lie—nothing but weakness and illusion. I told her first deaths should never be accepted; we had to fight them. I begged her to stop staring at the big house because madness and death might take hold of her as they had taken hold of Mrs Vermont.

For hours, I tried to fend off every memory that had made me who I was. I cursed my childhood and its ghosts the way a dying man curses his illness.

Then, once my fury was spent and the bottle empty, I started missing them.

All those characters.

And all that surrounded them.

The grains of sand crunching under my feet.

The salty breeze that dried my face, sending my mother reaching for the Nivea.

The nauseating but delightful taste of the ocean when you accidently swallowed the water.

The sun as it sank gently below the horizon, staring right at you knowingly as if to say, "We had fun today, but tomorrow will be even better . . ."

I cried for all of them and for myself. While the descriptions in the different chapters were mostly true to life, I filled in the blanks, remembering details the text had left out.

I saw that cursed and beloved bowl. The chimpanzee was wearing denim shorts, though the pages didn't mention them.

The air freshener hanging from the rear-view mirror in the Renault 5 gave me a headache when the windows were all closed. For many years, I was sure that my stepfather chose that fragrance on purpose. The text didn't touch on that either.

My mother had also had happy times, which weren't in the pages. I spent quite some time reliving them in an attempt to do her memory and her role as *my* patron goddess justice. The times we laughed together while watching a film. My smiles when I helped her make a cake, my face covered in flour and my fingers as buttered as the tin. Her hands stroking my hair as she read me a story, and how I would watch her sideways, misty-eyed, as I lay comfortably in my bed beneath the warm covers.

I cried for all those moments. The bad, of course, but also the good, because they were gone. They had left me alone with the cruel certainty that I could never get them back. They were all my first deaths. Even the hanged woman attended the funeral of my childhood. But I no longer saw her as a ghost hanging from a rope. Though I didn't have any real memories of the woman before her suicide, I imagined her beautiful and radiant, and her kind smile kept me company as the rays of the rising sun warmed my sad, exhausted face.

"A poem?" Samuel asked, clearly surprised.

He didn't look his best either. He closed the front door and followed me into the kitchen. While I tried to prepare some coffee (*Christ, where does Sarah keep the bloody filters?*), my best friend listened to my account of the night before, sitting in an aluminium chair at the black granite Eggersman counter, smoking his cigar.

"Yes, a poem."

"And you drank a whole bottle?"

"Twenty-year-old whisky, yes. And then I promptly threw it all back up over the balcony railing onto the sand. It looked like Rorschach inkblots. Funny, right?" I remarked bitterly.

"I told you to throw it out," replied Samuel with a sigh. He knew me well enough to know I was on the verge of losing it.

"Yes. You also told me to wait for you before reading the last chapter. Damn it, where are those bloody filters?"

"Forget it, just use your Nespresso machine . . ."

"No, I need a litre of coffee, not a tiny cup of espresso!" I shouted, spinning around to glare at Samuel.

My eyes stung. My throat, too. My whole body was in pain, actually. I was glad Sarah couldn't see me in my current state. *Maybe in this cupboard?*

"You didn't sleep at all?" he asked, watching me rifle through drawers and cupboards like a junky scrambling to find a lost hit.

"Nope. Not a wink. What about you?"

"A little, but not well. Maybe it's all bullshit, you know . . ."

"I'm not a kid any more, Sam. You don't have to reassure me."

As I spoke, a second wave of sadness washed over me. I stood there perfectly still, my hands resting on the counter, my back to Samuel, who got up and came to my side when he realized I couldn't hold it together much longer.

"We all need to be reassured now and again," he mumbled as he placed a hand on my shoulder, just like he had that evening years before when we'd both watched the fire. "Forget about the coffee. Take an hour for yourself. Go and take a shower and lie down. We'll talk more later. We're in no state at the moment."

I listened. Since I didn't have the strength to argue, I struggled up the stairs and lay down under the painting of the calm sea in which I longed to drown myself.

I woke up in a sweat and noticed muffled noises coming from below. I listened closely, thinking it might be Sarah's heels on the marble floor in the entrance hall, until I remembered our fight from the week before. I took a refreshing shower, choked down three migraine pills, and put on clean clothes before heading back downstairs, drawn by the smell of fresh coffee.

"In the cupboard on the left, behind the cereal," explained Samuel as he handed me a large mug. "And not a single drop on the rim," he added with a smile.

"How long was I out?" I asked.

"Three hours, but you'll need much more to get back on your feet."

"Thank you," I said as I took the coffee.

We sat down on either side of the kitchen island and drank in silence.

"I'm scared," I admitted after a while.

"Of what?"

"Of becoming a character."

"What do you mean?"

"As a novelist, I spend my time dreaming up characters. I dress them, choose their words and actions, and decide whether they live or die. I have all the power. But now I'm afraid I've become one of the characters. I feel like someone has rewritten my past without my permission. And the worst part is that it's really happening. I'm the main character in most of the chapters, and the author hasn't given me any reason for writing them. He hasn't even bothered to finish the story. I could make up my own story about the whole situation—characters trapped in a narrative, suffering as they wait for their creator to free them from it. But the writer would turn out to be dead, and the characters stuck there for all eternity . . ."

"Hmm . . . Writers becoming characters is nothing new.

Think of Paul Auster's *City of Glass*. But I'm glad to see your imagination is still firing on all cylinders!" joked Samuel as he blew out a puff of smoke from his overpriced cigar. "Well, in any case, it's my turn to be the main character now . . ."

"I'm listening."

Samuel pulled a few pages out of his jacket pocket and put them down on the counter. When I saw how wrinkled they were, I realized my friend had been through a similar experience to my own after reading this account of our childhood. Maybe he'd burned the rest. If so, he'd been braver than I.

"Is this your last chapter?" I asked.

"Yes. And it's not a poem. Believe me, I would have preferred one. Don't judge me, please," he warned. "I was a kid. I was muscly and knew how to feign confidence, but I was afraid of him. Just like you were."

Chapter 12

The Silent Man

August 1986

Samuel caught sight of his brother about ten metres away, on the other side of the safety barricades the firefighters had put up. Fabien was surrounded by colleagues from the factory and David's parents. They were all staring unblinkingly at the fire.

"Look, over there," he said to David, who was standing next to him. "They're all here."

Shadows and flames danced around the group's silhouettes, occasionally lighting up their malicious smiles. They were all watching the house, unable to look away, as if possessed.

Samuel understood that they would stay there, subjugated by the show before them until the flames died out completely. Not one of them would move a muscle before then. And he knew why. The satisfied smirk on Fabien's face, his puffed-up chest, and the way he kept his hands tucked in his jean pockets simply confirmed his suspicions. For the past several weeks, he had been certain his brother was plotting something. His strange behaviour . . . These "meetings" in place of the festive aperitif gatherings they usually attended on holiday . . . His silence during the few dinners they had actually shared . . . The stifled anger in his eyes . . . All of that should have alerted him sooner.

Even before coming to the seaside, there had been warning signs.

At school, kids had been whispering for weeks: "The factory is going to close. Our parents will be out of work. My dad said so."

But few of them had really believed it.

The factory had always been there.

"And Mr Vermont would never do that."

But then Samuel had watched as his brother came home angrier and angrier every evening. He could hear him through the thin wall between their rooms as he cursed the boss he had once praised. "That bastard will pay for this!" Fabien would shout as he slammed his door. Sometimes Samuel even thought he could hear his brother crying. But he wasn't sure and would never risk asking him. As usual, their parents pretended not to notice. They simply ignored their older son's distress. "Around here," their father liked to say, "a man has to learn to fend for himself." All while sitting comfortably at the table and letting their mother serve him his dinner. A contradiction in terms if ever there was one.

"Women, too," he would continue, taking out his pocketknife. "Everyone!"

"Even Nana Côte d'Or?" Samuel asked, thinking of his paternal grandmother who looked after him after school.

"I already told you not to call your grandmother that! Do you think she would have survived the war if she didn't know how to take care of herself?! Eat! He'll come out when he's hungry. Don't believe everything you hear about the factory. Old Vermont isn't like that. His father was an honourable man. And so is he. Pass me the wine."

"Okay, Dad," Samuel replied, though he glanced worriedly towards his brother's door, which remained shut despite the aroma of roast chicken and mashed potatoes coming from the kitchen.

Several days passed before Fabien's mood returned to normal. Samuel assumed it was because their holidays were coming up (this was ten days before leaving for Saint-Hilaire). He even convinced himself that this whole story about the factory closing was nothing more than a rumour which his brother had taken too seriously. Some quality time together would do them both good. Playing football. Sharing cigarettes without having to worry about hiding from their parents. Finishing Fabien's beers. Going to the Twisted Wood arcade. Listening to him tell the legend of the hanged woman and pretending (it wasn't much of a stretch) to believe it . . .

*

But as soon as they arrived at the bungalow on Avenue des Mouettes, his brother had become taciturn again as his bad mood returned. Then, on the first night, when Fabien came back from the meeting at David's place, Samuel had seen a wild spark in his eyes. A combination of determination and fear, he surmised. He listened to his brother's words without understanding them at the time. "We'll find a way, little brother . . . We know how to hurt him . . ."

But now, seeing Fabien smile like that as the boss's house burned, Samuel suddenly understood exactly what he had meant.

David told his friend he had to go. The group of adults was starting to break up, intimidated by the presence of a police officer.

"Me, too," replied Samuel. "If my brother catches me out here, he'll kill me! See you tomorrow!" He disappeared, breaking into a jog as he rounded the corner.

He sprinted down Avenue des Mouettes, then slowed, short of breath. He decided his brother would probably stay and hang around with his colleagues a bit longer. The deserted streets made him uneasy, however, so he walked at a swift pace. Normally at this time of night, there were plenty of people enjoying the last few minutes of cool evening air before heading inside. But tonight everyone is gathered around the boss's house, *thought Samuel, who would have liked to hear the occasional conversation or see a few tourists as he walked.*

He had the unsettling feeling that he was the last living soul in a post-apocalyptic world. As though the ghost neighbourhood had taken advantage of the diversion provided by the flames to expand its territory, muffling all sounds and suffocating any sign of life. Samuel tried in vain to push the terrifying vision from his mind. He imagined a snake made of sand slithering through the gardens, sneaking under the doors, slipping into the bungalows to extend its reach. When they got home, the holidaymakers would think it normal to feel the sand under their shoes. They would go to bed unafraid. None of them would imagine that once the lights went out, the sand scattered strategically throughout the house would regroup to form the snake's body once more, and that the sly reptile would then sneak up on them in their beds and take advantage of their vulnerability to imprison them for all of eternity . . .

Samuel almost broke into a run again. There was less than a hundred metres or so between him and the bungalow now. But first he had to go past the ghost neighbourhood and cross the road leading to the Mouettes Beach car park. He closed his eyes and tried to focus. In the distance, behind the abandoned houses, the waves crashed loudly into the sand, as if shouting a warning. Samuel tried to ignore them, the same way he ignored the threatening shadows of the empty buildings in the moonlit night.

When he reached the edge of the ghost neighbourhood, he heard a man's voice break the silence. Samuel stopped short behind a conifer hedge. The voice, which had gone quiet, as though its owner had sensed the boy's presence, seemed familiar. Samuel crouched down a bit and cautiously edged forward, being careful not to make a sound. His cheeks burned at the thought that Fabien might have seen him earlier. What if his brother had taken a shortcut to catch him red-handed and tell him off?

By the light of the full moon, Samuel slipped carefully into the alleyway perpendicular to the Mouettes Beach car park. His heart was racing. He just needed to make it across this alley and he could take refuge in the bungalow, under his sheets. He concentrated, focusing all his attention on any unusual noises he might hear. His first instinct told him to make a break for it. But if his brother was waiting for him, that would get him caught for sure. So, he stayed there unmoving for quite some time, leaning back into his leafy shield, hoping that the owner of the voice would grow tired of waiting. After what seemed like an eternity, he decided to head for the car park. Just as he was about to turn the corner, Samuel looked towards the ocean to make sure no one was hiding there.

That's when he saw them.

Two silhouettes, side by side with their backs to him, were making their way towards the car park.

The adult-sized figure was holding a child firmly by the arm. Samuel watched as they fled; he ducked periodically to avoid the nervous glances the adult kept throwing over his shoulder.

Where are they going? wondered Samuel, since he knew that there were no more houses on that side of the car park. He kept *perfectly still for several seconds, crouched in the shadow of the hedge, then stuck his head out one last time, hoping the path would be clear. "Shit,"* he whispered when he saw that the pair had stopped next to a car and were now looking in his direction. I can't cross the street to the alley until they've gone. I hope my brother—

He stopped abruptly.

He had just recognized the adult.

An ice-cold wind seemed to be blowing against him, making him shiver. Samuel prayed that he was mistaken. He tried to fend off the fleeting image his eyes had registered a second earlier, and which his frightened mind was now playing over and over in his head.

Despite himself, he looked back towards the two figures. He saw the streetlamp above them. His gaze followed the spectral light down to the adult's face. A scar appeared. And then he saw the hair. "Red," he whispered in a voice that seemed foreign to him, a voice that *had escaped from the abyss of his deepest fears. As his leg muscles primed to carry him away from the scene as fast as possible (he no longer cared if Red saw him or if his brother walloped him for not listening), a second revelation reached his conscience, knocking the air out of him and paralyzing his body: the child who had been trying to wrest her arm free. He had recognized her, too.*

Julie.

Samuel couldn't move. His mind was unable to assimilate the information his panicked senses were trying to relay.

Julie.

No, there's no way . . . Julie must be sleeping by now . . . It can't be her, *he reassured himself as the wind carried the mournful nocturnal sounds of the ocean to his ears. He closed his eyes tight and knelt down, praying for it all to disappear—the angry waves, the distant flames, Red, Julie, and even the hanged woman, whom he feared he would run into if he ever opened his eyes . . . He mumbled his brother's name. He hoped he would appear at the end of the alley, that he would bend down and take him in his arms. He needed his brother to comfort him, to shower him with love, the way Fabien used to when he himself was still a kid.*

Then, when Samuel finally stood up, still trembling, he saw that the silhouettes were gone. The car, streetlamp, and waves were calm now. Everything was as it should be. It seemed like nothing else had ever existed. Except for a vague, lingering feeling. Like the uneasiness you feel after a nightmare, when the monsters that were tearing your clothes and scratching your skin are beginning to vanish, vanquished by the light of day, although you can still feel their presence.

So, just as children convince themselves that an adult's violence is necessary or deserved . . .

Just as they convince themselves that ghosts aren't real . . .

And that the whispers are simply dying waves . . .

So Samuel convinced himself that this scene had never happened.

He walked home slowly, into the welcoming arms of elective amnesia.

And he yearned to become an adult soon, just like his brother.

August 1986

"You're hurting me," complained Julie.

"Be quiet, I heard something," urged Red, who was standing perfectly still. Then, after searching the darkness for a few minutes, he pulled Julie along towards the car.

"They burned down the house," she said, tears streaming down her cheeks. "Is it true what they say, about the hanged woman?"

"No, it's not true. It's just a story," lied Franck.

"What now?"

"I have to kill you. You understand, don't you?"

"Yes," replied the girl.

"Are you scared?"

"No. Will I become a ghost?" she asked, as a sudden spark of light appeared in her eyes.

"Yes. And you'll whisper in the ears of the living for many long years. Come now. It's time."

I was stunned by what I had just read.

As for Samuel, he was still and silent.

I no longer had in front of me the confident, loud-mouthed publisher who could sell the rights to a book for tens of thousands of euros, but a twelve-year-old kid full of guilt and shame. He had been the last one of us to see Julie alive. I envied him that. I hated him for running instead of trying to save her. In my anger, I persuaded myself that I would have reacted differently. There were so many possibilities: scream, go for help, jump on Red and make him let go . . . But no, Samuel had simply watched it happen, then kept quiet for all those years.

I slid the pages across the counter, trying to push away the feeling of disgust his final chapter had inspired in me.

"I'm sorry," he whispered as he fiddled with the paper.

And he clearly was. I had no doubt about that. But it was too late.

"Why didn't you say anything?" I asked, when I could finally articulate a response.

"I was a kid. I was scared. My whole world was collapsing around me. The hanged woman's house. Julie. Emilie. My brother. Everything that was important in my life was crumbling like sand statues in the wind. So, I stayed silent. Until now."

"But you must be the last witness to have seen Julie alive . . ."

"I know. And my last chapter confirms it. But think back to that night, David. Everything was so confusing. When my brother got home that evening, he immediately packed our bags. We still had two days of holiday to enjoy, but we left in the night, as did most of his colleagues. We fled the tragedy, tried to forget it. I honestly had no idea what had really happened. I had simply seen Red holding Julie's arm. It didn't prove anything. The police arrested the perpetrator the next day, and it wasn't him."

"Maybe he was an accomplice! If you had spoken up, even a week later— "

"Christ, David, I was terrified! Have you really forgotten how scared we were of that man? I couldn't move, I was petrified, and I was only twelve years old! Twelve! What did you want me to do? Fight him? So yes, I kept quiet. I became the 'silent man'. But don't blame me for it, David, especially not you! You know better than most that quiet children are the ones who have the most to say. But they're afraid. The way you were afraid to say that your stepfather hit you and your mum. And not only because you were afraid of what he'd do if he found out, but because you didn't want to seem weak! You only ever said anything about it if I asked you directly."

"That's not the same!" I argued.

"It's exactly the same thing! We were scared. We were kids. Silence was the only way out. And then, after the summer, there was the whole mess with the factory. Our families found themselves jobless overnight. The only thing anyone talked about for months was the factory closing. Everything else paled in comparison. We forgot everything else."

He was right. The next morning, my mother had packed our suitcases, too. Around ten o'clock I'd heard a knock on the door and had run down to open it, hoping to see Julie and Samuel. But instead, I found a uniformed police officer on the doorstep who asked to speak to my parents. My mother had welcomed him into the lounge, and I made my way back to my room to finish gathering my things, my heart broken at the thought that I wouldn't get to say goodbye to Julie.

Six years later, once she had divorced my stepfather and we had moved away, my mother told me the truth. I wasn't a child any more, so she felt it was time for me to know what really happened to Julie.

"Do you remember our last summer in Saint-Hilaire?" she asked as she sat down across from me at the table, cradling her coffee mug in her hands.

"Yes," I said, surprised she was talking about a time that seemed to belong to a previous century.

"You and Samuel made a friend . . ."

"Julie," I said so quickly it surprised both of us.

The memory of the friendship bracelet she had given me popped into my head. It hadn't lasted long—it had broken that winter.

"Yes, Julie," repeated my mother, her chin trembling.

"What about her? Why are you crying?" I asked.

"I'm all right," she said, wiping away a tear with the back of her hand. "Something terrible happened . . . I didn't want you to know before, you were too young . . ."

"What happened?"

"She was murdered."

"Murdered?"

"Yes. Now that you're old enough to understand, you should know. They found the perpetrator right away. He'll still be in prison for quite some time."

I tried to remember Julie as I finished my breakfast. I managed, but it was harder than I would have thought because the face of another girl—a girl from my secondary school with whom I was madly in love—kept interfering with my memories of the summer of 1986. The new girl's name was Stéphanie Boussère and we would share many "firsts"; she had been my official girlfriend for seven months at the time.

I was ashamed not to feel more when my mother told me. Julie's face seemed so abstract. My memories of her, her voice and blonde hair had lost their power and substance, carried off by time and the new emotions that were coursing through my teenage body and soul. I could recall certain scenes from that summer (the first time we met, the time she joined us and spread out her towel, our night at the arcade . . .) but the details of the rest of it had faded, leaving behind fuzzy memories. When I first realized I was forgetting (maybe two or three years after that summer), I had tried to retrieve my memories by going back through all of the different things we had done with Julie that week. I would lie on my bed concentrating hard, whispering her name again and again. At first, I would only need to say it once or twice for her smiling face to appear and utter the famous, "That really wasn't very nice". And then I would fall asleep. But over the course of months and then years, it took me longer and longer to bring the memories up to the surface. Until one day, when Julie's name kindled a barely recognizable shadow.

"This is all so stupid! Why would anyone want to make us relive this summer from our childhood? What's the point?" I protested.

"Guilt, David! My last chapter is laden with it! Whoever sent the text wanted me to feel guilty about Julie's death. But let me tell you, I've felt guilty for the past thirty years! I don't need some bastard to write it down for me! As for you, I don't know . . . Maybe they thought your books lacked poetic charm . . ."

His witty remark helped relax the atmosphere a bit. I made a quick trip to the lounge to get my cigarettes. The blazing sun shone on the French windows, through which I could see the small waves washing up on the shore. It seemed the sea had spent all of its energy during the storm the night before. When I turned my back on the ocean to return to the kitchen, I felt once again like I was being watched. I spun around, but there was only sea and sand as far as I could see. Nothing more. I studied the landscape for a moment, sure I would spot a desperate paparazzo. ("Depression strikes famous writer following separation," would be the caption of the photo.) But I was wrong.

When I returned to the kitchen and Samuel, he was smoking

his cigar again, filling the room with an acrid, animal scent. His shoulders were no longer slumped. His eyes no longer fled mine. *The businessman chased the kid away with a good kick up the arse,* I mused as I watched him rip up the pages and dump them into the Wesco bin.

"I'm going back to Paris," he said. "I have work to do."

"When?" I asked.

"This afternoon."

"But . . . Don't you want to know more? I mean . . ."

"David, I've had enough. I don't want to hear another word about it! It's all in the past! Emilie and Julie are dead, the guilty party was convicted, end of story! I got the message the arse-hole sent, loud and clear: GUIL-TY. All right, sure. But I don't care any more. And for the umpteenth time, you should forget about all this and come back to the present, too. I'm sorry, in any case, but I have to go. You're not the only author I work with—and the others don't go on and on about hanged women, murdered girls, and burned down houses."

"Who did you go and see?" I asked, curious. "On the phone you said you paid someone a visit . . . A ghost."

"Did I?"

"Don't play dumb. It was someone with ties to your last chapter."

"What about you? Weren't you supposed to wait for me to read yours?"

"Where were you yesterday?" I insisted, ignoring his sarcasm.

"Aah, you're such a pain in the arse!" he said, throwing his hands up in the air.

"You said you'd tell me about it," I pressed, moving closer to him. I had no intention of letting him off the hook.

"Forget about all this, David. Jesus!"

"No, it's too late to forget about it now. So, who was the ghost?"

"Goddammit! Fine, all right, but afterwards not another word about it! Okay?"

"Okay."

"I went to see him," said Samuel quietly.

"Who?"

"Red. I wanted to confront him. I wanted to get the answers I didn't get that night."

"Does he still live across the street from—"

"Nana Côte d'Or? Yes."

"And?"

"And he's vanished. He's a ghost now, too. That's why we have to let it all go, David. Everyone tied to this story turns into a ghost."

Samuel told me about his trip to our hometown.

He explained that he had parked in front of Red's house—the house we used to watch from the other side of Rue Camille-Desmoulins as children, from Nana Côte d'Or's courtyard. She used to watch us after school until our parents got off work. Samuel's paternal grandmother had lived alone since her husband's death (undoubtedly caused by the assault on his liver mounted by the moonshine eau-de-vie he distilled in the garage, where the smell alone could get you drunk). The nickname we had given her wasn't due to an unbridled passion for Burgundy wine (in fact, she didn't drink at all in a bid to spite the ghost of her alcoholic husband), but for another product, just as precious in her eyes: Côte d'Or dark chocolate.

"Nothing has changed," Samuel affirmed. "Red's house is as nondescript as ever. Four walls covered in crumbling stucco. A gently sloped roof. Green metal shutters, often closed, even during the daytime. Just like when we were kids. So, I summoned my courage and knocked on the door. I felt nervous and stupid because after all these years I was still full of apprehension at the thought of seeing him face to face. But I was determined. Determined to get answers to my questions. What was he doing with Julie that night? Why was he pulling her by the arm? Had he helped murder her? What about Emilie? Did he know her, too? I waited for a solid minute, then knocked again. Behind the house, the ruins of the factory blocked my view of the horizon. It's still standing, you know. The big chimney, the hangars, the main building . . . Just like before. Anyway, no one answered. I walked around to the back and looked through a dusty window. There were no signs of life. So, I crossed the street to say hi to Nana Côte d'Or. I hadn't been to see her since Fabien died, six years ago now.

After an hour or so of chatting, I finally asked her if Red still lived across the street.

'Why do you ask?' she replied. 'More coffee?'

'No thank you. There's no one home. The letterbox is over-flowing.'

'I know. The postman's worried, too. He's young. He has a nose ring. You know, like cows used to have.'

'Have you seen him recently?'

'Red? The last time was six months ago. One night in February. The tenth to be exact.'

'How do you remember the exact date?'

'I may be ninety years old, but I see and hear just fine, and though my memory may not be what it once was, it still works, too. Especially on important days.'

'What's so special about 10th February, Nana?'

'My goodness . . . It's your grandfather's birthday, of course! Chocolate is good for your memory. I should have given you more of it as a child! You and your friend. How is David, by the way? What's he done with his life?'

'He's the same, still a writer.'

'Right . . . I always said he was a lazy one . . . He wouldn't have lasted a single day in the factory . . . Not like your brother and father . . .'

'Okay, Nana. So, on 10th February?'

'It was dark. I had just finished dinner when I heard a car park in the street. I looked out the window and saw a man get out. I recognized him immediately. First off, because I had met him once before, at a Christmas party at the factory. You don't remember; you were still little. But also because all the factory employees used to take an annual picture with the boss.'

'Who are you talking about, Nana?'

'The boss, of course. Paul Vermont.'

'Are you sure?'

'Yes, that's what I'm saying. He still carries himself well, very elegant, though he didn't seem quite as sure of himself as before and his hair is greying now, but it was definitely him.'

'But it was dark.'

'Red put in a porch light with a motion detector. It turns on whenever someone comes through his gate. There was enough light for me to recognize him.'

'What happened?'

'Red invited him in. I did my washing up. I was surprised to see Mr Vermont around town since he'd left the area after that whole mess with the girl and all.'

'Yes, Nana. I remember.'

'When he finally left Red's house, they waved to each other and the boss got back in his car. That was it.'

'And you haven't seen your neighbour since?'

'No, not once. I talked about it with the postman and the butcher. They haven't seen him either. In town people say he must be dead. Maybe he heard voices, like Mrs Vermont.'"

"There, now you know!" concluded Samuel, already on his way to the door.

"What do *you* think?" I asked, still immersed in his story.

"I don't know, David. Maybe he's dead, maybe he moved. No idea. I did what I had to: I tried to make up for my mistake. I tried to trade my silence for a conversation with him. But it didn't work out. At least I tried . . ."

"Are you really going back to Paris right this minute?"

"Yes. You know me, I've had enough of the sound of the waves, the briny smell . . . I need my pollution fix! One last thing: according to Nana Côte d'Or, the boss moved, too. I don't know if it's a good idea to tell you, but apparently he doesn't live far from here."

"Where?"

"In Saint-Hilaire, where the pirates cry for his wife."

I was disappointed to see my best friend go, and disappointed that he didn't want to stay a few days longer to help me unravel the mystery. But I wasn't angry with him. I understood that Samuel had been living with a terrible secret since the tragedy. A reprehensible secret for an adult (because it was true that, if he had immediately told his brother or anyone else, Julie might still be alive) but an understandable one for a child (fear, that protean monster, which can manifest itself as a violent stepfather or a scary red-haired man and sneak up on us in a dark street, in our bedrooms, or whenever we hear a sound behind us).

I sat there for some time thinking about everything I had just learned. I hadn't made any real progress, but at least I knew what was in Samuel's final chapter.

The man and his silence had been set free by memories and words.

I decided to get to work on the text that had got the better of me the night before, when I was too sad and drunk to face it. I lit another cigarette and fetched my last chapter (crumpled on the lounge floor) and my MacBook. I googled the first lines of the poem and scanned the dozens of suggestions brought up by the search engine. I chose one at random and read the description.

But she was of the world, which fairest things exposes
To fates the most forlorn;
A rose, she too hath lived as long as live the roses,
The space of one brief morn.

Poem written by François de Malherbe, a French poet born in Caen in 1555 who died in 1628. "Consolation for Mr Du Périer" was published for the first time in 1607. It was a new version of the poem "Consolation for Cléophon", which he wrote in 1592, when his friend, Cléophon, from Normandy, lost his daughter Rosette. When the young Marguerite Du Périer died in 1598, Malherbe modified the original poem to express his sadness and condolences to the bereaved father, Mr Du Périer.

I thought for a while about the poem. I visited multiple sites about poetry, Malherbe, Cléophon and Du Périer, cursing them in turn for not providing a clear and obvious answer as to why these lines appeared in my final chapter.

The entire afternoon went by, but I still couldn't figure it out. My frustration was at its height because I was certain that this chapter would unveil the author's motive for writing the mysterious pages in the first place—as Samuel's had for him. I leaned against the balcony railing to think (noticing the gulls pecking at what was left of my vomit from the night before) and remembered that Samuel had said where Mr Vermont was now living. "In Saint-Hilaire, where the pirates cry for his wife."

I recited the poem in my head (I'd read the four lines so many times that I had memorized them) and repeated a sentence from the description of the text, which was also burned into my memory: "Malherbe modified the original poem to express his sadness and condolences to the bereaved father, Mr Du Périer."

Suddenly, it seemed obvious.
It couldn't be a coincidence.
Julie's father.
Saint-Hilaire.

"What do your parents do?"

"They're dead."

Samuel and I had believed her.

We had believed her because we had no reason not to.

When Julie told us both her parents had died in a car accident, neither one of us questioned her. But years later, right after my mother told me Julie had been murdered, while I was trying and failing to remember the details of her face, I realized it had been a lie.

"That's not all," my mother had said as I helped her clear the breakfast table.

"Mum, I don't really want to talk about any of this. She was just a friend, I didn't know her that well," I objected, desperate to flee Julie's ghost and seek refuge in Stéphanie's arms—we had planned to meet at the entrance to my building in half an hour.

"Wait," she pleaded. "I need to tell you the truth. It'll only take a minute. I just need to fetch something . . ."

My mother disappeared into her bedroom (I heard the door of her wardrobe creak) and came back a few minutes later with a newspaper.

"I kept it," she said. "I don't really know why. But here, read it. Afterwards, I promise I'll never mention Julie again." She handed me the paper, her eyes still rimmed with tears.

"There's no reason to get so upset, Mum, really."

"I know, I know, but . . . Right, look at the time, I have

to get to work. Don't forget the dishes," she reminded me without any real hope that I would do them. She kissed me on the forehead on her way out. "Say hello to Stéphanie for me."

I grabbed the newspaper and sat down at the kitchen table. I had no idea why my mother would have kept it all these years. The same way I had no idea why the topic upset her so much. I didn't understand her tears or her palpable sadness. Or her inability to look me in the eye while she was talking about it. I immediately recognized the photo on the front page: it was the old Vermont factory. Then the headline caught my eye: *Day of Mourning at Vermont Steelworks*.

As I read what followed, a dark anger began to grow inside me:

> *Today not just one man but an entire factory, an entire village, are in mourning. This afternoon, the owner of Vermont Steelworks will bury his daughter, Julie Vermont. The young girl was found dead last Friday on the beach in Saint-Hilaire-de-Riez, where employees take their holidays in a factory-owned residence. Nine years ago, another tragedy struck this same family, when the wife of the man everyone here respectfully refers to as "the boss" committed suicide. Though the Saint-Hilaire police quickly apprehended a suspect, nothing will ever be able to console Mr Vermont, who, like his father before him, is beloved by all. The paper offers its sincerest condolences. The funeral ceremony will begin in the village church at ten o'clock sharp.*

I couldn't believe it.

Julie was Mr Vermont's daughter.

When my mother came home from work that night, I peppered her with questions.

"Why didn't anyone know he had a daughter?" I asked.

"Some did. But we never saw her," she explained. "Mr

Vermont lived outside the village. It was rare to run into him anywhere outside of the factory."

"Still, she must have gone to school somewhere."

"When his wife died, the boss was too depressed to take care of Julie. She was only three at the time. Mr Vermont lost himself in his work seven days a week, his own version of therapy. He decided it was best to have Julie go and stay with Mrs Vermont's sister, who lived in Bordeaux and had the means and the time to take care of her properly. He visited her regularly. In the months after his wife's death, we would always ask about his daughter when we bumped into him at the factory. But his replies were always so full of sadness that we stopped mentioning Julie. Time went by. We had no idea what had become of her, but out of respect, we kept quiet . . . And in the end, we forgot."

"Did you know it was her? In 1986, I mean?"

"No. I had no idea Julie was in Saint-Hilaire," my mother assured me, looking away.

I was so angry with Julie.

Why had she lied to us like that? We were her friends. She could have told us the truth, and it wouldn't have changed a thing about our friendship. I thought we had been bound to one another, not just by a friendship bracelet, but by a deeper feeling, a feeling that had warmed our hearts as we stood on the beach, our clumsy young bodies navigating between fear and desire.

This lie, this incomprehensible deception was the last straw. Over the next few weeks, I did my best to completely erase my memories of our last summer in Saint-Hilaire. I threw all of the sentiments and the smiles, the feelings and the innocent happiness into the sea and watched as the fairy lights of the Twisted Wood arcade sank deep into the freezing ocean of my resentment.

I was eighteen years old.

A selfish age.

An age when we are desperate to cast off the last traces of childhood.

When we become deaf to the words of others.

Until the whispers of those faded memories come back to haunt us, years later.

He watched as the Mercedes left the property. It had arrived earlier in the day. A rather stout man had got out, followed by a thick cloud of smoke from the long cigar clasped between his lips.

The binoculars he was using weren't high enough quality for him to zoom in on the visitor's face. He saw him disappear into the house before he was able to study his features properly.

When the Mercedes passed right by him without the driver paying him even the slightest bit of attention (his car was carefully hidden behind a row of maritime pines), the man turned to gaze at the entrance to the property. Unsurprisingly, the electric gate moved, but was unable to close completely. The metal arms got stuck before they could unfold to their full length, as if held back by invisible forces.

That could come in handy, he had thought on the first day, when he noticed the malfunction. And ever since, each time he parked across from the house, he was amazed not to see a repairman at work on the problem.

He turned the key in the ignition of the hire car and, for the last time that day, drove slowly towards the entrance.

He'd been watching the house for a week now. Ever since the envelope had been dropped off. A woman had left with a suitcase early in the week. But since then, there had been no visitors, apart from the man driving the Mercedes he had spotted earlier in the day. That intrigued him. Either the person who lived in the house was a hermit, or they had no friends or family. *Given the situation, why repair the gate? Nobody came through it even when it was wide open,* he thought.

Located right on the beach, the villa should have been totally invisible to prying eyes. But since the tall, solid gate at the main entrance refused to close, he could keep an eye on any comings and goings from his spot behind the pines.

The day before, during a stroll in Saint-Jean-de-Monts, he had learned the identity of its owner quite by chance. He had dropped in to the nearest estate agent's and pretended he was interested in properties like it. An elegant young woman had answered that she couldn't reveal her client's identity—he was famous and sought above all to preserve his "creative privacy" (he felt a degree of personal reproach in her words and wondered if she was sleeping with him). But just a few steps away, in the same street, the owner of the local bakery was more talkative and provided all the information he needed.

"We don't see him often," she explained with a sigh. "He's in hiding. Artists . . . You know how they are."

"An artist?"

"Yes, an author! He writes 'thrillers', I think you call them. Hmm . . . Personally I can't help but wonder who wants to read stories about murders when reality is more than enough! Did you know that thirty years ago, just a few miles from here two young girls were killed! And I doubt anyone will ever write about them! Not exciting enough, I suppose."

The stranger felt his cheeks redden. He suddenly wanted to slap her. Hearing this stranger allude to Julie and Emilie disgusted him. He only wanted one thing: a name.

"So who is this mysterious author?" he asked.

"Are you a journalist or something? The kind who sniffs out celebrities no one else can ever find?"

"No, madam. I just want information about the year his house was built. I'm an architect and I'm really impressed by the property," he lied.

"David. David Malet. Ring any bells?"

He couldn't believe it. After all these years.

When he had seen the silhouette he'd been watching for

days place a brown envelope on the front step of the property, he never would have imagined the past would catch up with him like this.

Of course he knew him.

He'd known him since he was a kid.

David.

He knew his best friend, too. Fabien's brother, Samuel.

Julie's last two friends.

So that was it.

It all made sense now.

"No, doesn't ring any bells," he replied. Then he left the baker's and leaned back against a wall to catch his breath.

Images resurfaced in his mind. Images he usually only saw at night. But sometimes during the day as well, as a warning. As if to say: we're not just dreams. We're as real and frightening as a body hanging from the end of a rope.

As he drove past the open gate again, the man noticed a black four-by-four leaving the garage.

A wave of hushed words emerged from his memory.

Words spoken by a blonde little girl.

"Don't kill me. I want to see my parents again."

And words spoken by another.

"Will I become a ghost?"

And then by a little boy.

"Can you hold my hand to cross the street?"

No, Jérôme, I can't.

It's too late.

You're a ghost now . . .

It seemed so obvious now.

The presence of Julie's father in the region and the allusion in the poem couldn't be a coincidence. I convinced myself that Mr Vermont would help me unravel the mystery. In fact, who else could have written the text? Who else would have any reason to unearth the events that preceded Julie's death? Who else would want us to remember?

I opened up a new search window in Google and entered *Paul Vermont* followed by *Saint-Hilaire-de-Riez*. Nothing worthwhile popped up. I expanded my search to include neighbouring towns but got nowhere.

No Paul Vermont to be found.

A dead end.

Suddenly, a solution came to me in the shape of a name—the name of someone I had egregiously ignored the past few days: Sarah.

The estate agency where she worked handled most of the sales in Saint-Hilaire. If the former owner of the factory had purchased a home in the area, there was a pretty good chance Sarah or one of her colleagues could help me out.

I decided to leave my den and drive to Saint-Jean-de-Monts town centre. After checking my appearance in the oversized mirror in the bathroom (the bags under my eyes were darker than usual, but nothing a restless night couldn't explain away), I grabbed the keys to my BMW and went out for the first time in weeks. The sun welcomed me with a blinding smile that made me squint and regret my excesses the night before.

I drove my four-by-four along the country roads for a few miles, then made my way along the beachfront when I reached town. In the distance over to my left, beyond the sand and the waves, I could make out the rocky silhouette of the Isle of Yeu. I had been living here for twelve years and still had yet to visit the island. I promised myself that I would take Sarah once all of this was over. There were no doubt plenty of local art galleries over there where we could buy more enigmatic and ridiculously expensive works of art . . .

I drove around several times until a tourist freed up a parking space. I pulled in and got out of the car, putting on a baseball cap and sunglasses so I could remain incognito. On my way up Avenue de la Forêt, I stopped at a flower shop and bought a bouquet of roses, which the florist wrapped up as she watched me out of the corner of her eye. My disguise seemed to be working though as she handed me the bouquet and my change with a simple thank you and goodbye.

I walked the few remaining metres to Sarah's agency without looking up from the pavement. As soon as I stepped inside, a meticulously groomed man in a suit welcomed me with a singsong "Hello!" His toothy smile and bright eyes informed me that the young man thought I was a client. I had never seen him before. (I only ever met Sarah's colleagues at the agency Christmas party, at which I generally drank too much. It wasn't the best way to remember new faces . . .) I replied with a more loosely articulated "Hello."

"Welcome! How can I help you?" he continued, standing up from his desk.

"I'm here to see Sarah," I answered with a smile.

The man in the suit paused for a moment, sizing me up. I must have really looked in a bad way because as soon as I mentioned her name he replied in a severe tone, "Sarah? And you are?"

"Her husband," I replied triumphantly, removing my cap.

His complexion immediately shifted from fake tan to blush. His protective alpha male attitude disappeared, and he mumbled excuses as he held out his hand for me to shake. I took it quickly, to reassure him.

"I'm so sorry! We haven't ever met, and . . . I'm Jean. I'm new here. It's a pleasure to meet you! I love your books!"

"Thanks, that's very kind of you," I said encouragingly as I made my way to Sarah's desk where a picture of us was displayed in pride of place next to her computer screen.

Jean offered me a coffee (which I politely refused) and seemed to be waiting for me to say or do something that might justify the fact that he was rooted to the spot in front of me, undoubtedly trying to pierce the secrets of my creative imagination.

"How's business?" I asked to break the silence and make sure Jean hadn't suddenly fallen asleep standing there, his eyes still open.

"Pretty good. Well, it's summer . . . People don't buy in the summer, they buy *for* the summer. We've had a few visits, but this is our low season."

"Sarah?" I asked again.

"Right, yes! I'm sorry, I'm not used to talking to famous people, so I'm a little . . . She's in the back. I'll get her!"

Jean had just unwittingly summed up the main reason I didn't like to leave the house: when people recognized me—and it happened a lot—they suddenly grew awkward, stuttering and unable to speak, unsure of what to do with their hands. And rather unfairly, since I was in fact the victim of these strange situations, it always fell to me to restore normalcy. Sometimes by signing a book shyly handed to me, other times by smiling and agreeing to pose for a selfie that the stranger would later show their friends, bragging about chatting with me as if we were old pals. In those moments I dreamed of a world without fame. A world in which I hadn't written a single book. A world that had been gone for years.

Jean disappeared into the back and called to my wife in a

tone I found much too familiar, kindling a spark of jealousy. A few seconds later, Sarah appeared, and her smile quickly made me forget my childish reaction.

"They're beautiful!" she exclaimed as she took the roses. "I'm impressed you went into a shop without me!"

"Sarah, I'm sorry about all this," I said in a slightly over-dramatic tone, as I watched her colleague, who had taken refuge behind his screen, out of the corner of my eye.

She was wearing a perfectly tailored light-blue skirt suit that made her look far too good for a day at work in my opinion. The sweet, familiar scent of her perfume filled me with regret. Why was I neglecting a woman like this? Julie's dead body popped into my mind as the most plausible explanation. It was a brief vision, a fleeting neural quiver, but the resulting feeling was electric and long-lasting. The image disappeared, as if gently carried out to sea by the tide.

"Are you okay?" she asked when I took off my glasses. "You look exhausted."

"I'm all right," I replied unconvincingly with a shrug. "How are you?"

"It's not always easy to share your life with someone who lives with dozens of characters. Sometimes I feel like I'm less important than they are. But I knew that from the get-go, so . . ."

"I know. I . . . Again, I'm so sorry. I'm going to change. I promise. I'll listen to you and we'll go out more often . . . As soon as this is all over, I'll take you to the Isle of Yeu!"

"What do you mean when this is all over?" replied my wife with a frown.

Julie's corpse appeared again. Blonde hair fanned out on the surface of the water like jellyfish tentacles.

"Don't tell me you've still got your nose in those pages! I told you to let that nonsense go."

"I've almost figured it out . . . Give me a few days. I know I'm asking a lot, but I need a little more time."

"Jesus, David! This is becoming an obsession!" she exclaimed as she sat back against her chair with a sigh.

"I'm almost there, Sarah!" I pleaded like a child. "The poem, Emilie, Julie, the deaf man, the silent man, and the blind man . . ."

"David, I'm really starting to worry! What are you talking about?"

"I'm the deaf man in the story, Samuel is the silent man. The only person left is the blind man. And his last chapter will help us solve the mystery."

"My God, David, I thought you were here to apologize . . . Can you hear yourself? You sound like a madman!"

I shot a quick glance in Jean's direction. I wouldn't have been surprised to catch him nodding in agreement with Sarah's last assertion. But all I could see were his hunched shoulders hiding behind his computer screen. I realized that we were talking too loudly and lowered my voice as I leaned in towards my wife.

"Just a few days . . . I promise. I love you. Please trust me . . . Only a few more days."

"Christ! Why on earth did I marry a writer?! I'm coming home in three days," she declared. "If you haven't figured this all out by then and put it behind you, we'll be having a very serious discussion."

"Three days. Great. Fantastic," I mumbled, though she was giving me much less time than I had planned.

"David, have you been drinking? Have you seen your eyes?"

"No . . . Well, last night, yes . . . But I'm fine except for this migraine. Sweetheart, I need a favour."

"A favour? I'm confused, did you come here to apologize, to ask for more time, or for a favour?"

"It's important. Crucial even."

"What do you want?"

"Could you look through your client database to see if a man named Paul Vermont has bought a house in the area?"

"Paul Vermont?"

"Yes, that's it."

"David?"

"Yes, sweetheart?" I simpered.

"What is going on with you?"

"Nothing serious. Don't . . . Why do you ask?"

"Because you turn up here with a bouquet of roses, you're not making sense, and it seems like you got pretty drunk last night. And, yesterday, at almost exactly the same time, a man in his sixties came in here asking questions about Paul Vermont . . . And about you."

Suddenly I could see a house on fire as if it were actually there in front of me. People writhed in a madcap dance around it, as if to encourage the flames to climb higher and higher as the rest of the crowd moved dangerously close, exclaiming in admiration.

"A . . . a man? What did he ask exactly?"

"He wanted to know who owned the house."

"The house?"

"Our house."

"He had seen our house?"

"David, with the gate broken, anyone can see it from the street."

"Why was he asking?"

"He said he was an architect."

"You didn't believe him?"

"Let's just say he seemed a little . . . unpolished for an architect. And then there was this scar on his cheek. It gave me the creeps."

"Sarah . . ."

"Yes?"

"What colour was his hair?"

"Red, why?"

I slumped down into the chair behind me. A glass of water appeared almost immediately. I imagined Sarah's face, her incomprehension. Her words reached me like a faraway echo, like sentences spoken underwater. What was Red doing snooping around? Why was he after information about me?

After a few minutes, I swam back to reality. Sarah's voice became intelligible again.

"You're white as a sheet, David," she said worriedly. "It's like you've seen a ghost."

I managed to drink the water without spilling it on the agency carpet. My hands were shaking, but my wife didn't seem to have noticed. I could read the anger and disappointment in her eyes.

"It's just the heat and the drinking from last night," I reassured her. "It's nothing. It'll pass."

"Still, all this for a pile of paper you found outside our door . . . And now this redhead?"

"I've got no idea who that could be," I lied. I cleared my throat. "Could you help me out with Paul Vermont?"

Sarah stared at me for a moment, then sighed loudly. She typed the name and consulted the screen before printing out a document. On the other side of the room, Jean was sat perfectly still at his desk, immersed in his files. He was probably frustrated that he couldn't hear us any more.

"Here," said Sarah as she handed me the page from the printer tray. "His address. It's in Saint-Hilaire, not far from the Mouettes neighbourhood."

"Shit," I whispered when she mentioned the name of the holiday village from my childhood—the place where my childhood had ended. "I don't understand," I ventured as I folded the piece of paper. "I looked online but found nothing."

"Of course you didn't. He bought the house under another name. It's a common practice. All that matters to us is that the sale goes through . . . But we still have to keep the buyer's real identity on file for legal reasons."

"What name did he buy the house under?"

"You do know you're asking me to break a lot of privacy regulations, don't you?" she asked, raising an eyebrow.

"It's important."

Sarah sighed again, a clear indication of what she thought about my questions. I gave her the sweetest look I could, though I was unsure of the result. I doubted my eyes reddened by the alcohol and my sleepless night were the best showcase for my love. Nevertheless, she turned back to her screen and read me the name.

"Paul Malherbe," she said. "The deed is registered to Paul Malherbe."

"My God . . ."

"A thank you would have been more than enough," she replied sarcastically, her gaze full of reproach.

"I'm sorry, sweetheart . . . I meant thank you for your help and . . . Just a few days. Everything will be wrapped up . . ."

"No, David, not *a few days*," she corrected me in a biting tone. "Three days. That's it."

My legs nearly failed me once I was outside on the pavement again. I found a bench and sat down. I put my baseball cap and sunglasses back on and thought back through what I had just learned.

Red.

Julie's father.

Malherbe.

I had the terrible feeling that I was nearing the foot of a rainbow and would have to watch powerlessly as the ghosts from my past escaped from the earth. I felt the same fear described in the text when Julie, Samuel, and I started down the wooded path to the arcade. A childish fear. A fear I would have to confront.

I unfolded the piece of paper Sarah had given me and read the address: *Paul Vermont, 18 Avenue de la Corniche, 85270 Saint-Hilaire-de-Riez.*

I was certain that I had found the end of the rainbow.

Henri read the pages several times.

The cat kept jumping onto the armchair his owner was sitting in, but each time he left with a meow, tired of waiting in vain to be stroked.

The former police officer didn't understand what he was holding in his hands. Or rather, he didn't understand *why* he had it. Who could have left the envelope? And why? The last chapter surprised him: it was the only one in which he was the main character. What did it all mean?

Henri stood up and made his way to the kitchen. He opened the bag of cat food and filled Whiskas' bowl to the brim. The cat reappeared at the sound, his resentment forgotten.

"Don't wait up, Whisk. I have to go and find some answers," Henri said to the cat, who already had his head in the dish and seemed oblivious to his owner's presence. The man who was no longer a police officer needed to talk to a man who was no longer a child . . .

Red followed the black four-by-four until he realized where it was leading him.

When he saw it parked on the coast road opposite Paul Vermont's house, Franck turned his car around. He cursed David's stupidity but was impressed by his courage. He thought back to the kid he had known in the summer of 1986. How fragile he had seemed. The way he walked into a room as quiet as a mouse, as invisible as a ghost. The fear he had been able to read in the boy's eyes. Constant fear. A childhood fear—the kind we never really escape.

His stepfather had been the cause of most of it. Franck had known that at the time. They had been colleagues and they sometimes had a beer or two back at the flats. But though Red had laughed at his dumb jokes, ignoring the hesitant shadows of the mother and stepson who clearly disliked him, he knew all too well what happened once they were alone and the door was closed. And few people understood childhood fears better than him. Few people knew the inextinguishable pain of a poorly healed scar.

But now, parked on the road in Saint-Hilaire, not far from the cursed place where his world had been turned upside down, he wished that David had stayed that same fearful kid from all those years ago.

He wished he would look down at his feet, keep his distance from the adults.

Wished he would pretend.

Wished he would close the door and forget.

I took the same road in the other direction until I reached Saint-Hilaire, where I easily found Mr Vermont's house with the help of my sat nav. The air-conditioning blasted the inside of the car with freezing air while outside, kites danced in the sky defying the blazing sun.

The house, which was smaller and less imposing than I had imagined, enjoyed an unobstructed view of the beach. I took in the panorama for a moment and noticed that the sand stretched along the coast as far as the eye could see; nothing— not even the odd rocky outcrop—blocked the view.

Nothing but sand.

For miles.

I realized that from my house, which was further north, I could walk it in about three hours. Three hours of solitude, striding in time to the rhythm of the waves. But that would mean setting foot on Mouettes Beach. And finding out what had become of the bungalows from my childhood. Two things I had refused to do since moving to the area.

I stepped through the waist-high gate (which instantly conjured up images of the huge, rusted gate at the boss's former house), walked down the short path, and knocked on the door (which in turn rekindled memories of the ogival door and the dried-out plants clinging desperately to the building with their brittle claws.) After a few minutes, a man who was still taller than me despite his hunched elderly frame opened up and looked at me suspiciously. He was going bald, and his skin was so thin that I could make out every vein, as if he were peering out at me through a death shroud. His movements were slow and tired. He was clearly resigned to his fate.

"Yes?" he asked doubtfully.

"Mr Vermont? Paul Vermont?" I inquired.

"What do you want?"

"I . . . I'm sorry to bother you, but I was wondering if we could talk."

"Talk? About what?"

"About your daughter and . . ."

Mr Vermont took a small step backwards. He frowned and his eyes darkened. Shouts and laughter floated up from the beach behind me, emphasizing the heavy silence between us. It was easy to tell that the sounds of happy holidaymakers no longer held any sway over the old man. In fact, hearing them was clearly painful for him . . .

"My daughter?" he replied eventually.

"Yes. I'd like to talk to you about Julie."

"I don't know who you are, but you have no business being here. Leave before I call the police."

The door began to close. I didn't know how to put it, but I absolutely had to get through to him before he slipped through my fingers.

"I . . . I knew her," I mumbled, looking down at my feet. "I spent that last summer with her . . . We were friends."

The door stopped, then started to open again and Paul Vermont's face reappeared. I had finally piqued his interest.

"You must be David then," he said gruffly.

"That's right. How did you know?"

"That week, I called her every night. And every time she told me about two boys, her 'new summer best friends' as she put it. If I remember correctly, one of them was very curious and was always talking—Samuel, I think, or something like that. While the other—David—was more awkward and silent. So this all adds up."

Hearing Julie's words in Mr Vermont's mouth brought me a strange joy. For the first time in a week, I was being led to her by actual spoken words. I was not having to decipher cryptic sentences from the pages found on my porch or the vague memories those words evoked; memories which had found their way back through the rainbow but remained too tarnished and twisted by the passage of time to guide me. No, part of Julie was in this man and his memories. My lips stretched into a nostalgic smile as Paul Vermont invited me in.

It was delightfully cool inside. The elderly man invited me to follow him to the lounge. The shutters were all closed to keep out the heat. He opened them slowly and laboriously. The raw light chased away the gloom and I noticed a huge painting of an elegant woman hanging to the right of the entrance hall. I walked over to it, entranced by the calm, gentle face of the model.

"Eléonore," explained Mr Vermont. "My wife. Not long before the illness struck."

The portrait was surreal. Eléonore Vermont's blonde hair seemed to radiate light. It framed her face in a halo that must have been visible even in near darkness. Julie's face came to me then, just as pure and angelic as the first time we ever spoke. *The blonde hair seemed to absorb all the sunlight, turning it an even prettier shade of gold*, I thought as I stared at the painting. Behind her raged a furious sea, grey and tempestuous, that contrasted sharply with her serene expression. When I noticed that the portrait was signed by Eléonore herself, it seemed clear that Julie's mother had probably realized the illness was creeping in long before those around her did, and that the destructive waves were an unconscious projection of her inner turmoil. But another detail quickly eclipsed this train of thought. A detail so small that I had to lean in to see it clearly. In the background, to Eléonore's left, the mast of a pirate ship poked up discreetly between two waves.

"My wife loved to paint. She had a real gift," explained Mr Vermont as he pulled up a chair for me.

We sat down at the large wooden table. He offered me a

cup of coffee, which I politely refused. I was dying to light a
cigarette (I should have thought to smoke before knocking) but
fought the urge. It was clear that Mr Vermont's health was
fragile. Pill bottles were scattered about the room.

"Do you live here alone?" I asked.

"Yes. A nurse comes by every morning and I have a cleaner
in twice a week. She also does my shopping for me. A young
lady from Saint-Hilaire. A nice girl."

"Are you ill?"

"Like most old men," he joked with a shrug. "But I don't
think you came here to talk about my health."

"You're right," I admitted, still trying to figure out what
might be wrong with him. "I came to talk to you about Julie."

"Why are you interested in my daughter now, after all these
years?"

On the drive over, I had decided not to mention the text.
Too much was still unclear for me to divulge its existence to
anyone else. I still didn't know who had sent it to me or why.

"Well, it might seem strange, but over the past few days, my
memories of Julie have been resurfacing. She and Samuel and
I spent a lot of time together. I seem to remember that she told
us her parents were dead. I don't understand why she lied.
When I found out the truth, it felt like a betrayal. It didn't
match up with the frank, sincere girl I had known."

"She lied because I asked her to," Mr Vermont replied simply,
as though he'd been waiting his entire life to answer the question.

"You . . . You asked her to?" I repeated, perplexed.

"Exactly. No one could know that she was my daughter.
That was the rule."

"But why?"

"Because people are crazy, young man. And at the time,
they were even crazier than usual . . ."

"I don't understand."

"It's quite simple, really. I had made her a promise, and a
promise must always be kept. When her mother died, I couldn't

take care of her. Her aunt raised her in Bordeaux. She went to school there and I went to see her at the weekends and during her school holidays. Her aunt's housekeeper—Auntie, I believe you called her—took wonderful care of Julie. They became inseparable. There was no reason for Julie to live with her workaholic father who was blinded by grief and alcohol. My weekly visits were more than enough for her. She asked me only once to tell her how her mother died. She had just turned eleven. Telling her about her mother's fading memory and that she had committed suicide by hanging herself was out of the question. So, I made up a story: a sudden and unexpected heart attack during our summer stay in Saint-Hilaire. I told her that Eléonore hadn't suffered, that she had gone peacefully. Julie asked me again and again to take her back there, to the beautiful house where her mother had gone to sleep for the last time. I always refused because I myself didn't have the courage to go back. Then she made me promise. And when Julie really wanted something, there was no talking her out of it! I reluctantly agreed that she could spend a week in the Mouettes bungalows the following summer. I had never seen her so happy!"

When he mentioned that he had told Julie her mother had died of a heart attack, I realized that she had first learned the truth about her mother's death the night we went to the arcade. She had heard that her mother had hanged herself from us. We had been unwitting messengers of the worst possible news.

"But why couldn't she tell people she was your daughter?"

"Just before that summer, the factory had run into financial trouble. Major trouble. I knew that I had no choice—I would have to declare bankruptcy before the end of the year. If I remember correctly, your stepfather was a welder and your mother worked in accounts?"

"That's right. Do you remember her?"

"All of my employees were like family to me. Really. We celebrated every birthday. There was a bonus for every birth. And every time someone retired it broke my heart . . . And then, after Eléonore died, the staff became my lifeline. But there was nothing I could do. The news of the closure had been leaked and I'd been receiving threatening letters.

"What kind of threats?" I asked, intrigued.

"Oh, it usually wasn't much really. Just blowing off steam. But a few weeks before Julie was due to leave for Saint-Hilaire, a much more explicit and dangerous letter turned up."

"What did it say?"

"I remember it like it was yesterday. *You'll pay for this. We'll burn down your house and the ghost of your wife. And your little girl, too.*"

"My God . . ." I couldn't help but exclaim. "But you still let Julie go?"

I didn't understand why a father who knew his daughter was in danger would do nothing to stop it. If he was telling the truth, he was just as guilty as the murderer!

"They were only words. The words of frustrated men. And she wasn't alone. She had protection."

I listened as Mr Vermont explained that Franck, Red, the only person he truly trusted after his wife's death, had been in charge of looking out for Julie. He was the boss's eyes and ears. He was the one who worried most when the first threatening letter arrived in April 1986. Since he knew most of the employees and was unfailingly loyal to Mr Vermont, Franck had decided that he would find out who had sent it. He had suspicions about a certain group and deliberately got closer to them that summer, to gain their trust. Mr Vermont didn't name names, probably to spare my feelings, but I knew he meant my step-father, Fabien and the other people who had met in our lounge the night we arrived at Avenue des Mouettes. And my mother. Paul saw how troubled I was and quickly reassured me. "Sometimes people lose their way, son. And love is often what leads them astray. Don't blame your mother. She didn't really have a choice."

"So, Red was in charge of protecting Julie and keeping an eye on the people who wanted to hurt her?" I asked, pushing from my mind the idea that my mother may have been a part of it all. Unfortunately, every time I did, her strange behaviour, vacant stares, and contagious sadness came back like stubborn waves trying to dig the truth out of the sand.

"Exactly," replied Julie's father. "He reported back to me several times a day."

"But it wasn't enough . . ." I said with a sigh and a glance at Mrs Vermont's self-portrait.

"No. Unfortunately, it wasn't," Mr Vermont admitted sadly.

"What would you say if I told you that my friend Samuel remembered seeing Red with Julie just a few hours before they found her body?"

"I would say that that's perfectly plausible. He was probably taking her home. There was the fire, the crowd, and the death threats . . . He must have thought it best to walk with her. He would have told her he was going in the same direction anyway."

I studied the old man's face for a moment. It was dotted with age spots and hidden pain, but it still commanded respect. Nevertheless, I got the distinct impression that he was hiding something.

"Do you think that . . . That my stepfather and his friends really could have killed Julie?" I asked to hide my suspicions.

"No," he replied immediately. "They were afraid of losing their jobs. They were angry and undoubtedly drunk during most of their holiday, but none of them could have done it. They took their frustrations out on the house. And the murderer was arrested the next day. A local teenager who had no ties to the factory."

"What about Emilie. Was there a link there?"

"I have no idea. You know, children often disappear for no real reason. They're easy pickings. And the world is full of predators. Yesterday, on the radio, there was a segment on the topic. The reporter was talking about children who disappeared in Detroit in the late nineties. Many people thought it was the work of a mysterious giant of the mist, escaped straight out of an ancient legend . . . As for Julie and Emilie, a few oddballs believed that they had been summoned by the pirates. While you say your friend saw her with Red and you clearly imagine the worst of him. Don't listen to any of that nonsense. We know the truth. The murderer is in jail. Let Julie rest in peace. She deserves it. Forget the whispers."

"What whispers?"

"The whispers from the past, your memories! The ones you hear when you think of Julie, of your mother, and of that terrible summer! We all have forgotten memories that resurface from time to time, rekindled by a smell, a taste, a sound, or an event that instantly takes us back. Don't trust your memories or those of your friend. Sometimes they hold more suffering than comfort . . ."

Mr Vermont paused and looked at the portrait of his wife. I thought I could see his lips moving, as if he'd forgotten I was there and was speaking directly to the painting. I was convinced that once he was alone again, the shutters closed, he would stand and converse with her as naturally as he had with me.

"Do you believe in ghosts?" he asked me suddenly, turning away from Eléonore.

"Ghosts? No . . . No, I don't—"

"You should. This is all really one big ghost story. About the dead who come back to life . . . And about the living who are already dead . . . They're all ghosts. And they all have a message to share. Ponder that. Never forget it. Repeat it to yourself and keep it in mind before your memories become ghosts as well . . ."

"I'm not sure I understand . . ."

"There's nothing to understand. Let the dead rest in peace. That's all," he concluded impatiently. Then he stood up with a tight-lipped smile. "You know, going back through all these painful memories changes nothing, and it wears me out. I think it's time for you to go."

I stood up in turn and made my way towards the front door.

"One last question," I insisted as Mr Vermont opened the door and the warm air rushed in.

"I'm listening."

"Does this poem mean anything to you? 'But she was of the world, which fairest things exposes, To fates the most forlorn; A rose, she too hath lived as long as live the roses, The space of one brief morn'?"

Paul Vermont went pale. The light accentuated the whiteness of his skin.

"François de Malherbe," he replied, clearly shaken. "He was my wife's favourite poet."

Franck parked the car behind the row of pine trees.

Across the street, the open gate beckoned to him, inviting him in.

He closed his eyes for a moment trying in vain to ignore the whispers from the past. They were always there. They had been for years. Ever since the night when the Vermonts' home had gone up in smoke, followed not long after by Julie. Red had thought that with time, his memories would fade. But nothing can keep the past from whispering. Nothing. He slammed his fist into the steering wheel. He knew he had to act. He had to keep his promise. Always. Whatever the cost. He had to protect her. Even now.

He waited a few minutes for his mind to quieten down. He bitterly regretted how things had turned out that summer. He had almost learned to live with it when Paul Vermont had turned up at his door in the middle of winter six months earlier to let him know that the truth would soon come out. The old man had claimed that he didn't know where the leak had come from, but Franck knew him well enough to notice the deception in his voice.

And now it all made sense.

He had to act.

But he couldn't lose control.

He remembered David as a boy. He had grown to like him while looking out for Julie. He hadn't protested when Auntie told him they had become friends. He had actually been quite pleased.

"Let her have her fun," he had said. "She's a kid. Kids need friends."

"All right, if you're sure it won't be a problem," Auntie had agreed. "They seem to be nice boys."

"They do," Franck had replied, thinking of his scar. "But often good kids don't attract good adults."

"She's happy to be here. Mr Vermont did the right thing," Auntie reassured him.

"He kept his promise. Now I must keep mine."

Red had watched over the trio as they became inseparable. He had had second thoughts when he had seen them sneaking out of Auntie's bungalow in the middle of the night. He had followed them and looked away when Julie and David had paused on the beach, probably for their first kiss.

But the situation was growing ever more intense. David's stepfather, Fabien and the others were determined. They wanted to hurt the boss. They wanted to punish him for hiding the truth. The petrol cans were ready, as were their alibis.

But they were too cowardly to act. You could see it in their shifty eyes when the boy came into the room.

So Franck had volunteered.

He would kill Julie.

I left Paul Vermont's house with the uncomfortable feeling that I was missing something.

My wife's favourite poet.

Was Eléonore the key to unravelling the mystery? I refused to go down that rabbit hole. If I did, what would my next step be? Buy a Ouija board and try to reach her beyond the grave to get the answers her husband refused to give?

I was certain of one thing though: Paul Vermont hadn't told me the whole story. I had also noticed the way his mood had changed when I mentioned Emilie. That's when he had decided that he was in a hurry to get rid of me, as though I had touched a nerve—something even more painful and embarrassing than Julie's death.

My phone chimed to let me know I'd received a message. I pulled it out of my pocket and read the text from Sarah: *Three days*.

"Shit," I grumbled as I drove through my broken gate. Only three days to track down a ghost and get her talking!"

That's when I noticed a red Fiat Panda parked right outside the front door. The driver was still inside—a mysterious, unmoving silhouette. The thought that it could be Red (still a bogey man to me, and one who had recently inquired about my address) filled me with childish fear. I stopped the BMW and rifled in vain through the glove box, hunting for an object that I could use as a weapon to defend myself. (*Packet of tissues, no; old road map, not any better; clicker for the gate, nope.*) But as I anxiously opened the car door and the sound of the waves enveloped me in a final embrace, a very tall, thin man (*he really must be uncomfortable in that tiny car*) emerged from the Fiat and walked towards me. I dropped the Biro that I had been holding like a knife (I had thought that if I aimed for the eyes, I could probably get away from my scar-faced attacker) and got out in turn.

"This is private property," I announced, my voice tinged with empty bravado.

The man stepped closer and held out his hand with an awkward smile. "I know, Mr Malet, I hope you'll forgive me. The gate was open, and I decided it would be best to wait in the courtyard."

"Wait for me?" I asked, confused. "Did we have an appointment? Are you here to fix the gate? Did my wife call you?" I could hear the countdown in my mind: *tick tock, tick tock—three days* . . .

"No, not at all. I'm here because I think we share the same problem."

"What problem? I don't know what you're talking about. I'm quite sure I don't even know you . . ."

"I'm the blind man, Mr Malet. And I'm afraid you're mistaken. We've met before."

August 1986

Paul Vermont left his office around seven o'clock that evening.

He had worked late, calling every factory around in an attempt to find work for his best employees. But the economic slump had gripped the entire country now, and none of them could help.

He dialled the number of the bungalow where Julie and Auntie were spending the holidays, but there was no answer. Maybe they had gone out for ice cream with the two boys Julie was always talking about. Or maybe they were still at the beach, enjoying the last rays of sunshine . . .

When he got home two hours later, he was welcomed by the cheerful barking of Malherbe, the golden retriever Eléonore had adopted a decade earlier. The dog wagged his tail and ran alongside the car until it came to a stop in front of the comfortable house. Paul stroked his nose, wondering if he also missed his wife. Malherbe led the way to the front door and barked again, eager to lie down in the lounge and spend the evening dozing on the rug.

Mr Vermont sat at the table eating his frozen dinner and thought of how best to announce the imminent closure of the factory when they were all back from Saint-Hilaire. He had jotted down soothing expressions imbued with hope to express his regret and the inescapable situation they were all in, but the words seemed meaningless. He thought about his father, the "old man" as the employees had called him, at their summer barbecues—a tradition that had stopped the day he had found Eléonore hanging from the end of a rope.

Now the only source of light in his dark life was Julie.

She was looking more and more like her mother. She had her blonde hair and fine features, and eyes which hinted at unfathomable depths . . . He had hesitated before letting her go to Saint-Hilaire. But she deserved the chance to get to know the place her mother had loved so much. It wouldn't be an option any more once the factory closed. The banks would seize the holiday village to offset the company's debts. The money would be used to compensate the employees. He didn't imagine a bright future for the ageing buildings after that.

"Promise me you'll let me visit Saint-Hilaire," she had begged.

Mr Vermont instinctively turned towards the painting hanging on the wall in the dining room. "Eléonore," he whispered as he frantically wiped away the tears that were streaming down his face. "Can you see Julie from our house at Mouettes Beach? Is she smiling? Has she told you how much she loves and misses you? Isn't our daughter beautiful?"

Then Paul Vermont slowly cleared the table, his efforts mired in the lethargy that afflicts people who have lost all hope. He wished his dead wife goodnight and climbed the stairs to his bedroom.

At two o'clock in the morning, the phone roused him from sleep.

He had been having a nightmare in which his wife, dressed only in a nightgown, was wandering, lost and confused, on a dark beach. The full moon cast a malevolent glow and there were voices coming from the sea. "Do you hear them, Paul dear?" she had asked in a voice he barely recognized.

"Hear what, Eléonore?"

But she didn't seem to hear his answer. She kept walking and the seafoam soon caressed her ankles. Then her knees disappeared and the water climbed rapidly to her waist.

"The voices," she said as she moved further from the shore. "They're calling me . . ."

Paul was unable to move. He was rooted to the spot, standing on the sand, watching helplessly as his wife walked out into the sea.

"The voices, I must reach them. They need me."

He stayed there unmoving until his wife had completely disappeared. The final image he retained from the nightmare as he rushed down the spiral staircase to the phone, which had been ringing for several long minutes, was of the sea. Just after Eléonore had disappeared into the waves, the ocean had become as calm and smooth as a mountain lake.

"Hello?"

"Mr Vermont? It's Franck . . . I . . . I . . ."

"Jesus, Franck, spit it out! It's two in the morning. What's happened? Is Julie all right?" Part of Paul was still asleep on that beach.

"Mr Vermont . . . Something . . . Something terrible has happened . . ."

A rush of rage transformed the lake back into a stormy sea.

13

"We've met before?" I asked, confused.

"In 1986," replied the stranger. "I was a police officer. I'm the one who found Julie's body. My name is Henri. Henri Bichaut.

"I see . . . Hello Mr Bichaut," I replied as I shook the hand he held out to me. "And you say you're the 'blind man'? I don't understand . . ."

I had had enough strange encounters for one day. I don't know if it was Red's presence in the area, the odd feeling I had when I left Paul Vermont's house, or the countdown imposed by Sarah, but all I wanted to do was go inside, take an aspirin and forget about the whole thing for a few hours.

"I'm sorry to be so suspicious," I said as I studied Bichaut. His scruffy beard, shifty eyes, worn trousers, and sweat-drenched T-shirt, not to mention the fact that he had illegally trespassed on private property, didn't compute with my idea of how a police officer should look and behave. "I just don't know what you're talking about."

Henri Bichaut seemed to understand my doubts. He pulled some folded pages from his back pocket. "I received these a few days ago," he explained. "You're the main character. The deaf man. So I guessed you had probably received the text too. But if that's not the case, I apologize for bothering you . . ."

"Wait . . . I did. And so did my best friend, Samuel."

"The silent man?"

"Yes, the silent man. Come inside and we'll talk."

We made our way towards the porch, but as soon as I set foot on the first step, I realized that the front door was open.

My entire body froze, causing Bichaut to instinctively follow suit.

"What's going on?" he asked.

"The door. It's open."

"Your wife?"

I wasn't the type to discuss the torments of my love life with a stranger. I simply shook my head.

"You don't have an alarm?" he asked.

"We do. But since I rarely go out, I always forget to turn it on."

"Do you want me to go first?" offered Bichaut.

"No," I replied in a voice I hoped sounded determined. I turned my head and caught sight of a rock big enough to be threatening. I picked it up. "Let's go."

We cautiously made our way up the steps, walking as slowly as astronauts in zero gravity. I willed my hand not to tremble as I pushed the door wide and stepped inside, followed closely (very closely—I could smell his sweat) by Henri.

"Do you have any enemies?" he asked. "Maybe something to do with your books?"

"Shush! Do you have a gun?"

"A gun?! I haven't been a police officer for years! Why? Do you have one?"

"No, just a black Biro in the car . . . On three we go for it, okay? At least we'll have the element of surprise."

"Uh . . . Okay," Bichaut replied succinctly. It occurred to me that, given his lack of confidence, it was probably best for the general public that he was no longer with the police. "One . . . Two . . . Three!"

We stormed in shouting indecipherably, our words mingled with onomatopoeias, the meaning of which was lost even on us. But the din was met with silence and then an echo.

"There's no one here," declared the former police officer.

"Well, not on the ground floor," I countered. "I'm going to have a look upstairs. Stay here."

I climbed the stairs carefully, visited each room in turn, then came back down without having found a thing. "Nobody up there either."

"Christ, what a mess!" exclaimed Bichaut.

The lounge, whose walls were usually home to overflowing bookcases, were now completely bare. The bookcases had been thrown to the ground, scattering hundreds of books all over the room.

"I think the bloke who did this must have been looking for something," suggested my trusty Watson.

"Looks like it. And he must have found it. Otherwise he'd have ransacked the other rooms, too."

"Do you own anything particularly valuable? A safe?" asked Henri.

"Look around," I said. "The Bang & Olufsen TV unit is worth three months' worth of minimum wage alone . . . The Mac is still here. And thank God, so is the photograph in the master bedroom. Any normal thief would have pillaged the wine fridge in the kitchen, too!"

I let my mind wander for a moment, imagining Sarah coming home the next day and making her way to the bedroom to find a Eurocamp advertisement where her Hiroshi Sugimoto piece should have been (rather funny, really), and discovering that the thief had made off with all of our other valuables as well. A thin layer of cold sweat swept over me affectionately. I decided then and there to have the gate fixed as soon as possible.

"We should call the police," said Bichaut.

"No, not yet," I replied. "Did you hear anything while you were waiting outside?"

"No, nothing at all. I stayed in my car until you pulled up. Have you read them all?" he asked as he plucked Albert Camus' *The Fall* from the floor.

"Yes. I spend my days reading and . . . Wait."

"What is it?"

"The manuscript."

"What manuscript?"

"The one you received, too. Well, my copy of it. I left it here on the table."

"Do you think . . .?"

"Help me," I ordered.

We spent a good fifteen minutes searching the room, lifting up bookcases and shifting through books, but we came up empty-handed. The person who had broken into the house had clearly left with it. I suddenly knew who the culprit was.

"Red," I finally said aloud.

"You mean . . . The man from that summer?"

"Yes. He's been in the area. He spoke to my wife yesterday. He wanted my address."

"I know I'm repeating myself, but I think you should call the police," insisted Bichaut.

"No, not until I've figured out what it all means. What is your last chapter about?"

"Finding the body and the investigation that followed."

"Can I read it?"

"If you like. What about yours?"

"A poem."

"Of course, perfect for a writer," he said sarcastically.

"Do you like cognac? I don't have any more whisky," I explained as I made my way to the bar. If I had been alone, I would undoubtedly have lost my cool and screamed in anger like I had the night before. But Henri Bichaut's presence made that impossible. From watching him, I was confident that he knew no more than I did about who had sent the envelopes. And like all ships—even those lost far out at sea—this ship needed a captain . . .

"No thank you," he replied. "I don't drink."

"Really?" I asked, surprised. "But you must be divorced at least?"

"Uh, no. Just single. Why?"

"No drinking, no gun, no ex-wife to bash . . . You would make a terrible character in a novel!"

"And you would make a terrible housekeeper," he joked as he gestured around the room.

"Before I start cleaning this all up, come with me out onto the patio while I savour this delightful cognac and read your last chapter. Because, believe it or not, I really think it will provide the answers to our questions."

"All right," agreed Bichaut. "I'll smoke a cigarette and watch the sunset. A nice change from my flat!"

"Ah, I knew it! We're saved. The cops always smoke in detective novels!"

Chapter 12

The Blind Man

"Snap out of it, Henri! What the bloody hell is on the beach?"
"I think . . . I think it's . . . Emilie."

The night had been a sleepless one for Henri Bichaut.

His boss as well as the firefighter, Pierre Mathieu, had followed him to where Emilie's body lay. They had also been sick upon seeing the burnt girl huddled in the foetal position.

They had contacted the inspector, who had alerted the superintendent. An hour later, the perimeter was locked down with a dozen rather agitated public officers inside. Generators fuelled powerful spotlights that made the detectives' shadows dance across the sand like holidaymakers on a summer afternoon. The paramedics performed an initial assessment of the body while Henri gathered the clothes folded next to the victim. With gloved hands, he had placed the evidence in plastic bags and handed them off to forensics. Then he had nodded to his boss, and finally stepped over the safety cordon to leave the crime scene and return home.

3:40 a.m.

In his bedroom, he had swallowed an entire Valium, certain that Emilie's corpse would still haunt him throughout the night.

Henri waited for the sergeant to break the silence.

The girls' parents had left the station over half an hour earlier.

The words spoken by Emilie's father still seemed to be floating around the interview room. The atmosphere was as thick and heavy as a threatening cloud.

"*No, this isn't Emilie's either. She never wore a friendship bracelet. I'm sure of it.*"

"*The Little Gregory affair.*"

"*I'm sorry, Sergeant?*"

"*You remember the Little Gregory affair two years ago, don't you?*"

"*Yes, sir,*" Henri replied, eager to see where his boss was going with this.

"*The mistakes made by the police, the different leads, the revelations in the press . . . Well, that's exactly what the superintendent doesn't want this time. In other words, he wants us to find the person who killed Emilie quickly. We can't mess this up and it can't take ages. He made that very clear on the phone this morning. And now I have to tell him that the body we found last night might not be Emilie but another child.*"

"*The coroner might give us more to go on . . .*"

"*Right . . . Or maybe the murderer will turn himself in,*" the sergeant replied sarcastically as he stood up.

The two men left the room with their heads hung low. Each at his own desk, they spent the next hour trying to understand. The coroner would be working on the autopsy now, at the morgue. The brand new forensics team had spent hours analysing the crime scene, but the defeated looks on their faces in the early hours of the morning hadn't boded well.

Around eleven o'clock, as Henri fought off exhaustion with an umpteenth cup of instant coffee, the desk officer waved him over to reception.

"*Bichaut?*" he asked.

"*Yes,*" he replied, in a thick voice.

"*You were down at Mouettes Beach last night, right?*"

"*I was.*"

"*Then this is for you.*"

"*What is it?*"

"*A call. A jogger who was out for a run this morning along the beach. He says he's found some children's clothing in the water.*"

*

Frédéric lived in Saint-Jean-de-Monts and went running along the beach to Saint-Hilaire and back twice a week. "It takes over two and a half hours," he explained. "I'm a gym teacher at the secondary school. I'm training for the local triathlon."

"Is this where you found the clothes?" asked Henri.

"Yes. I had just passed the part of the beach where . . . Where the police search was."

Henri turned towards the north. He could just make out the yellow tape that would cordon off the crime scene until the forensic results were back. Henri could also see the beach towels dotting the sand around the area and the curious tourists questioning the officer on duty for details before making their way to the water, where their thoughts returned to that evening's barbecue. He sighed resignedly and felt the sun warm his face for a moment.

"Right, good," he replied, adding that Frédéric might be asked to come down to the station to sign a statement. "Thank you for calling this in."

"Glad to help," said the jogger. Then he slowly disappeared into the distance.

Henri put on a pair of plastic gloves and squatted down next to the T-shirt which the waves had washed up onto the beach.

The superintendent doesn't want another Little Gregory affair, *he thought.*

He sighed again and unfolded the fabric to get a better look.

Rips in the front and back. Dark stains that could be blood. Shit.

He turned the T-shirt over and found writing embroidered into the inside of the collar. The name and last initial had probably been sewn in before the girl left for summer camp or on a school trip.

Emilie D.

Not far from the T-shirt, Henri found a pink sock which had been brought in by the tide as well. He found the same embroidered name inside.

Emilie D.

As in Emilie Dupuis, who had been missing for a week now.

Emilie, who was still missing despite the body found the night before.

Henri put it all in a large plastic bag and studied the horizon. He wondered if these two messages in a bottle were a call for help or a death sentence.

Emilie's parents came back to the police station that afternoon. They easily identified their daughter's clothes. Her mother had embroidered her name in them before a school ski trip. This time, the glimmer of hope that had still been very much alive in their eyes that morning went out.

Henri stayed in the room alone.

The sergeant was on the phone with the superintendent. Henri and his boss had just brainstormed ideas about what needed to be done: call a crisis meeting within the hour, send the clothes to forensics for analysis, contact the maritime unit in Les Sables-d'Olonne and ask them to send a team out to patrol the area, gather possible eye-witness statements from tourists at the marina, and study the currents . . .

Henri, like everyone who'd grown up on the coast, knew that if there was a body, they wouldn't find it until the ocean decided it was done with it. If it ever did. Sometimes the sea kept what it took. He also knew that after just two days in the ocean, bodies became unrecognizable. The water temperature played a crucial role (the warmer the water, the faster the body decomposed) but carnivorous crustaceans like crabs and lobsters could also speed up the process. Sometimes, after all that, the sea brought what was left of the body back to the surface, anywhere between three and seven days later. And the victim, missing one or more limbs, would emerge, its skin waxy and grey, like a battered doll.

Water and fire, *thought Henri as he tried to find a logic to the tragic events.*

But he was too tired to think.

When he stood up, he felt like he hadn't slept for an eternity.

*

Twenty minutes later, the desk officer received a second call pertaining to the missing girls. This time, he didn't dare interrupt the man on the line, who began to dictate instructions. Once he'd hung up, he hurried to the sergeant's office, but it was empty (the poor man was being raked over the coals by the superintendent), so he turned to Henri, who was resting his head on his desk in a bid to soothe the pounding in his skull.

"Henri?"

"Yeah?"

The desk officer was as white as a sheet. Henri watched as he held out a piece of paper with a trembling hand.

"An anonymous caller . . . He says he knows who we're looking for . . . He told me their address and where they work . . . The person who killed those girls . . . He says there's evidence in their car . . ."

14

Henri watched my face for a reaction. The gentle, rising moon seemed indifferent to the situation. The stars appeared one by one—eternal spots dotted like pixels over the night sky.

"This is how you found the murderer?" I asked in disbelief.

"Yes, thanks to an anonymous tip from a phone booth in another area of France."

"But the evidence was strong enough to charge him and put him away?"

"We found the rest of Emilie's clothes under the passenger seat as well as an empty petrol can in the boot. And the suspect had no alibi. He said he closed up at the Twisted Wood and then drove around and went for a walk on the beach to watch the full moon."

"The Twisted Wood?"

"Yes. Olivier was the manager of the arcade. A kid from Saint-Hilaire. At the time he was only eighteen."

"I knew him," I replied, thinking back nostalgically to the teenager who had introduced us to arcade games.

"Me too," replied Henri. "We went to secondary school together."

"Jesus, I can't believe he . . . No one had any doubts about his guilt?"

"My superior, the superintendent, and the judges were all certain of it. He was convicted and is still serving his sentence. He'll be out in six months."

"You don't seem to agree with them," I said as he blew his smoke upwards.

"You could say that," he replied, turning towards me. "I don't know why he couldn't account for his whereabouts, but I'm sure he didn't do it. The judges didn't pay any attention to a detail that seems to point elsewhere."

"And what was that?"

"The night before the fire, Olivier felt like he was being followed, or at least watched. He said that when he walked to his car after closing the arcade, he had seen a silhouette hiding in the car park. He didn't have any proof, of course. It was just a feeling. And it didn't carry much weight given the evidence against him."

"Why didn't he deny it? If he was really innocent, he could have just said he was at home!"

"Because he's Olivier," replied Henri with a sigh. "Incapable of lying and awkward with everyone except for the kids at the Twisted Wood. And he was under a lot of pressure, after all. Don't forget that the ghost of Little Gregory was hanging over us all. They needed to find the perpetrator quickly to prevent any more bad press from embarrassing the criminal justice system. It played an important role in the verdict. He was the perfect fall guy. Imprecise, hesitant, fragile . . . The case was quickly forgotten. The next year, the tourists returned. They sunbathed on the beach where Julie's body had been found. They swam in the ocean where Emilie's remains still lie. Do an internet search. You won't find a single line about any of this. No one ever looked into these tragedies. The town, the region, everyone wanted to forget—no one wanted Saint-Hilaire-de-Riez to become infamous for a double murder. Not a single cloud was allowed to darken the coastal skies. Olivier is all that's left of the story."

"You seem to like him."

"We were friends, and we still are. I'm the only person who visits him in prison," explained Henri.

We stood there for a few minutes without speaking. The waves cadenced the silence—a gentle and continuous litany for the two girls. And a potentially innocent man.

"What about fingerprints and DNA evidence?" I asked.

"There weren't any fingerprints," replied Henri. "The police determined he must have used gloves. And as for DNA testing, it didn't exist in 1986."

"A dead end."

"Afraid so."

I took a sip of cognac and tried to sift through the flood of information Henri's last chapter had provided. Then I compared it with the other two. I immediately developed a theory. I wasn't sure I should share it with Henri. The only person I fully trusted was in Paris, far away from this mess, and his parting words had warned me to forget about it all. But I knew I couldn't figure it out alone. There were too many details, too many unknowns. And I was running out of time. Sarah would be home in three days . . .

I stood up to serve myself another glass of cognac. I poured another glass as well and handed it to Henri.

"No, still no," he said.

"Toast with me, Henri," I insisted. "I think I now know why the three of us received those envelopes."

He stared at me for a moment, trying to decide whether I was serious or just crazy. In the end, he took the glass.

"Cigarette?" he suggested.

"Yes, thank you."

"I'm listening," he said once he was settled in a deckchair on the patio.

"The three texts were identical except for the last chapter."

"Right."

"So we can deduce that if there are clues to be found, they must be in the final chapters."

"Seems likely."

"Let's leave my chapter out of it for now. It's still just a poem to me for the moment, as meaningless as an equation in quantum mechanics."

"I've never liked physics," joked Henri. "Or poetry. So that's fine by me."

"Samuel's chapter tells us that Red was with Julie not long before she disappeared."

"Red? Him again?"

"Yes. And yours describes how the investigation led to Olivier's arrest. The anonymous call, the incriminating evidence, the pressure from the high-ups due to the Little Gregory affair . . . Should I continue?"

"I see exactly where you're going with this. But if you're right, why not just write, 'Olivier is innocent. Red murdered them'?"

"Because the person who wrote this wanted to gain our trust. They wanted to prove that they knew what they were talking about. An accusation without any context would have ended up in the bin. But this, this is different. Each of us read the pages over and over again. Samuel thinks that the person who sent the manuscript wants us to feel guilty and realize the terrible mistakes we made."

"I agree with that," said Henri.

"Yes, but that's not the most important message. You said Olivier is scheduled for release in six months?"

"That's right."

"Don't you find it strange that we received all of this just before he gets out?"

"I don't know . . ."

"It's so obvious! Samuel was totally wrong! It wasn't to remind us that we each should have had the courage to listen, to speak out and to look, and that we were responsible in some ways for what happened! That's not why the author wrote these pages! It's all so clear now that you're in the picture!"

"I'm afraid I don't follow, my friend. What do you mean?"

"What I'm saying is that the person who wrote this wants us to find the real murderer. That's the message!"

"So, Red?"

"Well . . . Our last chapters are the key. If we were to draw a conclusion from your two chapters, yours and Samuel's, it would undoubtedly be that Franck is the murderer and Olivier is innocent."

"But?"

"But I still haven't figured out *my* last chapter. And I'm sure that it holds part of the truth, just like yours. It will all be clear once I decipher it."

"Okay, well then, for now, let's focus on who could have sent the manuscripts."

"The first person that comes to mind is Paul Vermont," I said. "He called Julie every day. She could have shared details about me and Samuel."

"It was probably someone who was close to all three of you. Maybe someone who was watching you . . ."

"Wait . . . Paul Vermont had received threatening letters because his factory, where the holidaymakers at the Mouettes bungalows worked, was about to close. So he asked Red to watch over his daughter and make sure she was safe. Franck must have been watching her all the time, and us with her . . ."

"If Red wrote these texts, then your theory about why falls apart. He wouldn't have done it to inculpate himself. There are much easier ways to confess to a crime. What about your mother?"

"She died. Of cancer."

"I'm sorry. Your stepfather?"

"Not smart enough. Wait . . . Of course!"

"What? Who are you thinking of?"

"Someone who was never far off that week and who was very close to Julie. They were inseparable as Paul Vermont put it. Why didn't I think of her earlier?"

"Who?"

"The housekeeper, Auntie!"

Henri stared at me, as uncomprehending as a fish pulled from the water on a hook. "Auntie?" he managed finally. He was clearly sceptical.

"Of course! Julie must have told her everything . . . That's why the details are so accurate. Who was close enough to Julie to know that Malherbe was her mother's favourite poet? Who was close enough to her to hear all about her two new friends and to ask questions the answers to which would inspire her text years later?"

"What about when you snuck out to the Twisted Wood arcade? How would she have known? She was asleep!"

"Red would have told her. He must have followed us that night. She knew all about the promise Franck had made to Mr Vermont. Auntie must have known that Red was with Julie before she disappeared. Just as she must have known that Olivier had nothing to do with it."

"We have to find her then," urged Henri, nearly knocking over his glass.

"What?"

"Auntie. We have to find her and ask her why she wrote this."

"I . . . I don't know her name or where she lives. You didn't call her in when Julie's body was found?"

"No. Paul Vermont took care of everything. He came in that afternoon to tell us that his daughter had disappeared the night before. We immediately made the link with the burned body on the beach. He also identified his daughter's clothes. He turned into a ghost before our eyes. Parents shatter like china when you take their children. I watched it happen that day. I watched his soul crack and then crumble into dust."

"And we've come full circle. Back to Paul Vermont. He's the only one who can tell us more. And I know he was hiding something this afternoon. We'll have to go back."

"Tomorrow morning?" suggested Henri.

"If you're free?"

"Works for me. The only thing I have planned is to force myself to drink this cognac. I'm sure it will help me sleep. I'll spend the night here . . ."

"Here?"

"Yes. If Red or anyone else decides to drop in again, it will be easier for two drunk men to fight him off than one. You never know, maybe the Bang & Olufsen caught his eye . . ."

"Watch out, now you really are a detective straight out of a crime novel!"

15

Franck read the pages again, his eyes reddened by sadness and incomprehension.

After breaking into David's house (when he closed his eyes, even after all these years, he could still see the kid with his hunched shoulders, and the urge to teach his idiot stepfather a lesson was still there), he went back to the cheap hotel where he had been staying for the past few days. Sitting on the bed, where the *CSI* team armed with luminol would undoubtedly have found an astounding number of stains from various bodily fluids, he tried to contain his panic.

He stood up and paced the room, stepping carelessly on chocolate bar wrappers and empty biscuit packets from the vending machine in the lobby.

Why? Why?

Why bring Emilie and Julie back to the surface after so many years?

And yet, deep down, he knew the answer.

A truth he refused to admit. Paul Vermont had warned him six months earlier, when he'd come to see him at his house. He had told him that they wouldn't be able to keep the ghosts from whispering as Olivier's release date neared. "People will finally know what really happened in the summer of 1986 the day he leaves prison," Paul had added. "You should disappear, before they come looking for you. That's what I came here to tell you tonight."

As soon as his visitor had left, Franck had panicked, as he was doing now in his hotel room. He had packed two suitcases, cut the gas and electricity, and left through the back garden in the middle of the night, because he suspected—actually he *knew*, his neighbour was always at her window, even late—that the old woman across the road would immediately alert the neighbourhood if the automatic porch light came on.

At first, he had planned to head south, to stay with a distant cousin.

But as he left his native region, now plagued with unemployment and scarred by the carcasses of abandoned factories, he had felt the need to go back to the holiday village one last time.

He had driven through the night. It had taken four hours to reach Saint-Hilaire. He parked in the deserted street on the edge of what used to be the ghost neighbourhood but struggled to make out the houses that had once been there. The sand—a monster that neither time nor the wind seem to wear down—had almost completely devoured the buildings nearest the ocean.

It was a cool, quiet night and the sound of the waves in the distance greeted him like an old friend after nearly thirty years apart. The bungalows from the former holiday village were now little more than ruins, their windows broken, their walls a canvas for graffiti, and their roofs covered in moss. He knew the story, which Mr Vermont had shared. When the factory had closed, the holiday village had been seized and put up for auction by the municipality. A potential buyer had expressed interest, but he backed out once he realized how much it would actually cost to renovate it all. A second buyer, a Dutchman, had thrown his hat in the ring with plans to demolish the complex and build anew. The contracts were signed, but once again, the transaction failed to go through due to obscure procedural irregularities. Ever since, the company, headquartered in Amsterdam, had been fighting the town hall and regional government to obtain damages, damages which the small local authority would never be able to pay.

In the meantime, no one took any notice of the bungalows along Avenue des Mouettes, which rapidly fell into disrepair.

The village, which had once been so full of life, was now as silent and forgotten as a cemetery.

Franck walked down the paths, which were overrun with vegetation. Despite the many years that had gone by, he could have found his way through the maze with his eyes closed. He reached the boss's old house. Three walls still stood, but the fourth, of which only the bottom half remained, leaned dangerously inward as though it was being pulled by a force in the centre of the building. All the doors and windows were gone and the roof, part of which had burned that night, was now but a memory.

Still as a statue at the gate, Red stared at the thick crossbeam that shot up out of the ruins like a broken bone from a gaping wound. His face contorted in pain as his repressed suffering and sadness escaped: disrespectful teenagers had hung a rope weighted by a slipknot from the beam. He imagined the local kids coming to visit the "hanged woman's house" for an adrenaline rush, listening closely for whispers spoken from beyond the grave. He could see them taunting one another: "Bet you're too chicken to put your neck through the rope like that crazy old lady . . ."

A drawn-out sigh escaped from his tortured soul.

He thought about removing the offensive symbol. But he was fairly certain that it would be swiftly replaced. The house had become the mausoleum of a ghost who belonged to the locals now. In fact, they had scrawled a message in spray paint over the front door: *Hawnted house. Touch the rope if you dair!*

"Ignorant morons!" he shouted, as dismayed by their poor spelling as he was by their lack of respect.

Franck closed his eyes. He wished he could apologize to Eléonore as he had to Mr Vermont. Explain how his promise had got away from him and taken him to the point of no return. He wanted to tell her the things he had only told one other person—her husband. How he had failed to keep a promise once, and how much it had cost him.

The act he had regretted every day since he was a boy.

But it was too late.

So he turned around, walked back to his car, and disappeared to the South of France.

About five months after he had moved in with his cousin, a lavender farmer in Provence, he received an anonymous letter. As he read it, he thought back to the threatening letters David's stepfather and his friends had sent to Mr Vermont. But this one was devoid of violence. Instead, it told a terrible truth: *The boss is ill. He only has a few months to live. It's time to say your goodbyes.*

So Franck had driven back to Saint-Hilaire and parked in front of a smallish house on Avenue de la Corniche. As he opened his car door, he saw someone come out of the house. Someone he recognized instantly. And their presence here wasn't a good sign. He decided to follow the person, just for an hour or so, before heading back to say goodbye to the only friend he'd ever had. That's when he saw the familiar silhouette drop a thick brown envelope on the porch of a large house with a broken gate. Then another, in a letterbox located in the lobby of a block of flats.

And ever since, he had been holed up in this seedy hotel trying to understand.

Franck tried again to calm down.

No one will believe this version. The criminal justice system won't want to tarnish its reputation by opening a case it closed too quickly decades ago. Calm down. Even in the worst-case scenario, you'll have time to get away . . .

Red stopped pacing the room and sat down at the foot of the bed. Just a few minutes before, he had received a call from Paul Vermont.

"A certain David came to see me," explained Julie's father. "I think you know him."

"Yes."

"He's quite close to uncovering the truth. If he's at all clever, and I rather think he is, he'll figure it all out any day now."

"I . . . I'm not ready, boss . . ."

"We both knew this day would come . . . We were crazy to think we could keep it a secret for forever."

"Maybe there's another solution . . . I took the manuscript from David's house. I could do the same for the other two."

"What other two?"

"It says in the text that the manuscript was sent to three people. There's even a poem, which I'm pretty sure I've heard before. Maybe your wife . . ."

"Franck, we have to prepare ourselves. You can't keep the truth from coming out! It's too late."

"Boss, I did my best that night . . . I did my best."

"I know, but you went too far. That was not the promise we made . . ."

Then the line had gone dead. Mr Vermont had hung up, fully aware of how his last words would impact Franck.

Red yelled in anger and threw the receiver across the room. He covered his ears to block out the voices of the ghosts from his past, which were growing ever louder . . .

"Can you hold my hand to cross the street, Franck? Will you hold my hand?"

"No, Jérôme, you're big enough to cross on your own now."

"Let's race, then!"

16

The next morning, I woke up around eleven o'clock.

Henri had slept in one of the guest rooms on the ground floor. When I came downstairs, I found him opening and closing cupboards in the kitchen.

"There have to be coffee filters here somewhere! I doubt Red would have taken those," he grumbled.

Despite the cognac and the thousands of questions going through my head, I had fallen asleep surprisingly easily. I hadn't been startled awake by a single nightmare.

No hanged woman or pirates trapped at the bottom of the sea.

No scarred faces.

No burnt or drowned bodies.

Nothing.

Just a calm, restful night.

About as unexpected as coffee filters kept behind the cereal.

"In the cupboard to your left, behind the box of muesli," I said as I walked in. "Don't ask why. Sarah has her own logic when it comes to organizing the kitchen."

"Do you like it strong?" asked Henri with a smile as he placed a filter in the machine.

"That would be great. Did you sleep well?"

"Like a baby! Despite the slight headache due to that cognac you made me drink . . . I made sure to lock all the doors last night, but I couldn't get the gate shut."

"There's some sort of electrical problem," I explained with the confidence of a knowledgeable handyman, as if I'd actually looked into it.

I sat down and waited for the coffee to brew.

"And here you are, without a single drop on the rim, of course!" said Henri with a laugh.

"You're full of surprises, officer."

"I'm not an officer any more . . ."

"I know, I know . . . But part of me will always see you as the police officer who knocked on our door that morning in August."

"I understand. We're both still partly the people we left on that beach," agreed Henri. "Did that really happen?"

"What, you coming to our door?"

"No, the scene with your favourite bowl."

"Yes. It did."

We sat in comfortable silence for a while. We were like two shipwrecked sailors clinging to flotsam, rocked by the tide that took us in and out, between the past and the present, unsure when we might set foot on dry land again.

"I met your neighbour this morning while I was smoking out on the patio," Henri said finally.

"My neighbour?"

"Yes, the woman with the dog. She waved from the beach."

"Did you wave back?"

"Of course," he said, showing me.

I felt a twinge of jealousy. A bit like the one that had reared its head at the estate agency when I heard Jean call Sarah's name.

The old woman.

I had forgotten all about her. She had probably mistaken Henri for me. Given the distance, it was hard to really recognize someone. But Henri had done what I had been unable to do for the last few weeks. It was silly, but I had convinced myself that the moment we shared when she walked by on the beach was ours. Just like a teenager waiting for the ideal moment to kiss his first girlfriend for the first time, I had put off waving.

"You make money off your physical and social stagnation," Sarah would have chided me upon seeing my disappointment. "I've said it so many times. I'd be better off with a guy like Jean. He would have taken me to the Isle of Yeu ages ago . . . Look at that sad face, as though he's stolen something precious from you . . . Poor thing, the woman waved at him and not you . . ."

"Are you okay, David?"

"Uh, yes. I was lost in my thoughts, sorry."

I chased my wife's imagined criticism from my mind (though Jean remained present for quite some time, a stupid smile on his face . . .) and took a sip of coffee.

"I think you're right," Henri continued. "I thought about it before going to bed and again this morning. Auntie must be the author of the manuscripts. We have to find her and ask if what's written in Samuel's last chapter is true. If Red really killed Julie."

"You're thinking like a real detective now," I replied with a smile as I lit a cigarette. *(Don't forget to air out the house for at least three hours before Sarah comes home,* I carved a reminder into Jean's face with a knife.) "Let me take a shower and call Samuel to catch him up on the latest developments. He'll try to convince me this is all a waste of time, but at least he won't be able to say I didn't tell him."

Half an hour later, showered, shaved, and refreshed, I finished my call with Samuel. I was, of course, met with the famous, "It's all in the past, forget about it", but I sensed he was interested when I mentioned that Red was in the area.

"David, I probably don't need to say this, but he could be dangerous . . ."

"I know, but don't worry. Henri seems to be up to the task. He's a real pro," I lied to keep my friend from worrying too much. "In any case, I don't think he'll come back here. He found what he was looking for."

"Auntie . . . Why didn't we think of her right away?" Samuel wondered aloud.

"Because she was always so discreet," I replied, trying to think back to the number of times Samuel, Julie and I forgot her presence altogether as we played on the beach, only metres away.

"Maybe . . . Listen, one last piece of advice: if Red does come back and you feel like things are getting too . . . complicated, then you and John McClane have to go to the police, okay?"

"Okay."

After a twenty-minute drive, we parked outside Mr Vermont's house. We hadn't put together a very precise plan but we had agreed that I would talk and Henri would watch the old man's face for clues.

The door opened after a single knock, as though Mr Vermont had been standing behind it waiting for us. As I followed Henri into the house, I got the uncomfortable feeling that I was being watched.

I didn't just think someone was watching me.

I *felt* it.

Like an invisible hand on my shoulder.

I turned around to try to figure out where the feeling was coming from. I looked across the hot tarmac to the other side of the street and the sea beyond but didn't notice anything out of the ordinary. A steady stream of tourists spilled onto the beach, like on most days in the summer months. Their bodies were reddened by the brutal sun as they leaned slightly forward to gain traction, cursing the hot sand that burned the soles of their feet. They all hoped to find the beach deserted, only to be forced to share it with hundreds of other holidaymakers just like themselves.

And then there were the children. Children surrounded by balls, and kites, and light. Children whose parents kept a lax eye on them, blissfully unaware that years ago two girls had run along this same beach but had never left . . . *Are the sun's rays looking for the two little bodies the moon failed to protect?* I wondered as I watched the children dive into the sparkling sea. *Or are Henri and I the only ones still thinking about them?*

17

Parked behind a beach hut, Franck watched as David and his mysterious friend followed Mr Vermont into the house.

Apparently, his warning hadn't been enough. The "kid" had come back to ask more questions. With another person in tow, this time.

He'd have to take things up a notch.

Make them forget about the whole story.

Red glanced at the hunting rifle stored in its case on the back seat.

He didn't know if he would have to use it, but the possibility didn't frighten him in the slightest. After all, he had killed before to keep the truth buried.

"Please, sit down." Mr Vermont didn't seem surprised to see me. I suspected he may have purposefully kept things from me the first time to make sure I would come back. All of a sudden I felt like his puppet or a pawn on a chessboard, like I wasn't calling the shots.

Eléonore's portrait seemed to be watching us from the wall. It seemed different this time. Darker. More nefarious. More inscrutable than the day before. Maybe the half-light was the cause (the shutters remained closed this time and the room was lit only by a wan, spectral glow from the chandelier). The atmosphere inside the house was more like a dusty mausoleum than any place fit for the living.

"Mrs Vermont painted it just before her death," I informed Henri, who seemed to be hypnotized by the portrait.

"Not very cheerful," he noted. "Rather glum, actually."

"You're right," I replied, wondering if Eléonore had already decided to hang herself when she painted it.

Ten minutes later, Paul Vermont came back from the kitchen with a tray. He was slow and hesitant but refused our offers of help. I expected to see him stumble at any moment, his balance compromised by the weight of the tray, but his emaciated body reached its destination safely and put everything down on the table.

"I'm surprised to see you again," he said as he handed me a cup of coffee. "I thought we'd said all there was to say."

"I still have just a few questions," I replied, trying not to make him feel attacked. "And we're sure you're in the best position to help us."

"Who exactly is 'us'?" asked Mr Vermont. "I feel like we've met . . ."

"We have, Mr Vermont. I was a police officer back then. I'm the one who found your daughter's body."

"Ah . . . But you're no longer with the police?"

"No," Henri replied awkwardly. He didn't dare confess that it was Julie's death that had pushed him out the door.

Mr Vermont seemed relieved by the answer. The dusty clock chimed quietly. Julie's father walked slowly to the coffee table and picked up a blue pill box. He came back to his chair and sat down, letting out several quiet groans, then began carefully counting his tablets. I realized at that moment that the former factory owner wasn't just ill—he was dying. His eyes were faded, and I couldn't even tell what colour they had been when his wife was still alive and happy. His bald skull seemed as fragile as a newborn's and his wrists were skin and bones, threatening to break with each movement.

"If I may, Mr Vermont, what ails you?" asked Henri who must have read my thoughts.

"Time. The past. Memories. And a disease that has progressed much too far to be cured. These pills are buying me time, nothing more."

We respected his decision not to name his illness. We watched in silence as he took his medication. I suddenly remembered the man who had handed out gifts to all of the staff's children at the Christmas party. Every year, the families were invited to the factory for the event. The place was decorated with streamers and colourful Christmas trees. Mr Vermont would offer each child a sincere smile and a few words as he handed him or her a gift much better than our parents could afford. We admired him back then. He stood tall and we thought he was as solid and indestructible as the factory's chimney.

Once he'd swallowed the last pill, Paul closed his eyes for a moment. When he opened them again, it was to look at Eléonore. He smiled at her and his eyes seemed to lose themselves inside the portrait. When they emerged a minute later, they were veiled by the effects of the drugs. We understood that day would soon turn into night for Mr Vermont since his eyelids were already beginning to droop, like the curtain falling at the end of a show. Had he waited for us to arrive to take his medicine and avoid our questions? It seemed likely.

"Mr Vermont," I said eventually, "I lied to you yesterday. I didn't just start remembering. Someone made me remember. Someone wrote a text about that sad summer of 1986. And it would seem that the courts condemned the wrong man."

Henri's face registered surprise at my direct approach. But Julie's father would soon be unable to answer our questions. I couldn't waste precious time beating around the bush.

"I know, my boy," he confessed with a smile that clearly cost him much effort.

"You know about the manuscript?" I asked, surprised.

"Yes. But I thought you were the only one who received it."

"Why didn't you mention it?"

"Why should I have? You're the one who turned up on my doorstep with questions. You know, at my age, I don't care much about questions or answers. I am content to just watch and wait. But I gave you some precious advice. Advice you seem determined to ignore."

"Advice?"

"Yes. I told you not to listen to the whispers from the past, to ignore the memories."

"What whispers? Please don't talk to me about ghosts again . . ."

"The whispers that are between the lines. The memories stirred up by the wind."

"I don't understand . . ."

"You received much more than a text. The words were written by someone who is very much alive, but it is the ghosts who are speaking to you."

"I told you, I don't believe in ghosts . . ."

"Of course you do. You're just waiting to see one to admit it."

"No, I—"

"Alzheimer's didn't kill Eléonore—her memories did."

"I'm sorry, what?"

"My wife didn't kill herself because of the illness. She hanged herself because of the voices that tortured her soul, whispering in her mind all summer. The memories killed her, with their whispers and ghosts. Memories are dangerous for people whose minds are slowly going, because when they come back, as they did for my wife, you know they will be ripped from you again. Eléonore spent all of her childhood summers here. All of her most cherished memories occurred on this beach. She also loved tales of pirates."

"The drowned pirates forever trapped on their sunken ship," I mumbled, thinking back to the story Fabien had told to scare us.

"Exactly. Alzheimer's is a vicious disease. It's not when it holds you close that it hurts, but when it lets go for a moment. My wife only heard the whispers from the past when the disease loosened its grip. When she was fully present, she remembered the young girl she had been and the stories of pirates she had read. Then, when the disease drowned her mind again, the memories she no longer understood became voices calling to her from the ocean. That's why she hanged herself. To keep her memories intact. To save them from the abyss. Now do you understand what I mean when I say that listening to the whispers from the past can be dangerous?"

Henri said nothing. He listened, as we had planned. But it was more than that. He seemed to be completely absorbed in the old man's words. His eyes darted from our host to the portrait of his wife and back again, following an invisible path. I realized that the former police officer must have believed the legend of the hanged woman as a child. Maybe he believed it still. Maybe Julie and Olivier weren't the only reasons he left the police. Believing in ghosts must clash with the pragmatic attitude of the forces of law and order.

"Mr Vermont . . . Did you write these pages?"

"No, my boy."

"It's Auntie then, isn't it?" Henri asked softly.

Paul Vermont's eyes flashed to life for a millisecond, confirming our suspicions.

"Why?" I asked. "Does she know who really killed them? What if Franck killed your daughter?"

"You'll have to excuse me," replied Mr Vermont, "but my pills are beginning to take effect. I'm afraid I'll have to cut this discussion short."

"Why didn't she just say who did it instead of turning her accusation into a novel?"

"Sometimes, saying or even writing the truth isn't enough. You have to prove it. You have to push people to understand it to ensure it's irrefutable. Whoever wrote this wants you to understand the bigger picture before handing you a name. That's the only way to establish the truth."

"Then why give me this indecipherable poem?"

"The poem you quoted yesterday? Is that the one you mean?"

"Yes. Each copy of the manuscript has a different final chapter, which is crucial. My last chapter is this poem.

"David, I could tell you that Franck killed my daughter. But I could also tell you that your mother struck the match that set her on fire . . . Or your stepfather. Each of them is guilty in their own way. The only real truth is hidden in the lines of that poem you don't yet understand. Read them again. Look for the dead. As well as the living. If you really want to know the truth, you'll have to learn to believe in ghosts. There's no other way."

PART THREE

Whispers of madness

"The murderer isn't necessarily the only one responsible for death.
There are also those who encourage him."

August 1986

"Mr Vermont . . . Something terrible has happened . . ."

Paul Vermont was paralyzed. In the background on the line he could hear the waves struggling furiously against the sea bed, as though battling a terrible nightmare. Or perhaps they were grieving for the child whose body lay on the sand, fighting with all their might to gather her in their arms and erase an anomaly that should never occur on a beach—or anywhere else.

"What . . . What do you mean, Franck?"

Without realizing it, he had sat down in the mahogany armchair next to the phone. It had taken him a moment to articulate his question. He hadn't wanted to say the words out loud. He instantly regretted it. Just like he regretted allowing Julie to go to Saint-Hilaire.

"Please, Dad, let me see the place where she was so happy. Let me visit Mum's house . . ."

"On one condition, sweetheart."

"What?"

"Franck will go with you."

"Franck? The one with the scar?" Julie asked, surprised.

"Yes. He'll keep an eye on you. And if he decides it's time to go at some point, you follow him no questions asked."

"He scares me," she admitted, looking down at her feet.

"You have nothing to fear," her father reassured her.

"How did he get that scar?"

"It's a terrible story, Julie. I'm not sure that—"

"Come on! Please, Dad!"

As she always did when she really wanted something—whether it was a new dress, to have a friend stay the night, or to see the last place her mother had visited—Julie stared into Paul's green eyes for a long while with her head cocked slightly to one side and a sad, pleading look on her face, as if he had already said no. Julie knew that her father almost always gave in. *I'm just asking him for a story this time, shouldn't take long.*

And she was right. He bent down towards her and kissed her cheek, then whispered in her ear.

"I'll keep this short: when he was a child, he didn't keep a promise he made. And someone punished him for it."

"That's it?" she balked. "A scar for a broken promise?"

"Yes, sweetheart. That's all I can tell you at the moment. And don't bother giving me those big eyes again. I won't say another word," he chided with a smile as he stood up. His daughter was stubborn (a trait inherited from Eléonore, the most stubborn woman he had ever met) and he knew that she would ask more questions about the scar someday. But she was too young to hear the full story now.

Of course, it wasn't that simple.

Tragedies never are.

"He's too scary," pleaded Julie. "I wouldn't be comfortable with him."

"In that case, let's compromise. Auntie will stay with you, but Franck will never be far off. All right?"

"Okay, Daddy. You're the best. And look!"

"What?"

"It looks like Mum's portrait is smiling, too. I'm sure she loves our plan."

"I'm sure she does."

"What do you mean, Franck?" Paul shouted this time, cursing the sobs he could hear on the other end of the line.

Malherbe had woken up at the sound of his master's voice. He came and sat at Paul's feet, lowering his ears anxiously.

"They're dead, boss. I killed them both!" spluttered Red, letting out a deafening cry of anguish.

"Wh . . . What do you mean *they're* dead, Franck? What the hell happened?"

"I wanted to protect her . . . But they burned down the house and wanted to hurt her . . . I had no choice . . ."

"Where's Julie?" Paul asked, forcing his voice to remain calm though he was anything but.

"She's with Emilie, boss. They're both ghosts now."

"Emilie? Tell me where you are. I'm on my way . . . Tell me where Julie is!"

"There's no need. I'll come to you. I'll explain everything . . ."

"WHAT DID YOU DO TO MY BABY?"

The line went dead.

Franck had hung up.

Paul Vermont dialled the bungalow where Auntie and Julie were staying. His hands were shaking. Big tears rolled down his cheeks. His lips wobbled in pain and incomprehension. *No, it's all a mistake. I misunderstood. Julie is fine. She's made a friend called Emilie. Yes, that's it. I misunderstood, because of my nightmare, because of that terrible dream . . .*

But no one answered. He ripped the phone from the socket and threw it across the room with a shout of rage. It slammed into the wall just a few centimetres from Eléonore's portrait and crashed to the floor with a clang. The rotary dial came loose and rolled across the floor of the lounge.

"Are you happy now?" Paul shouted at his wife. "What do the whispers say now? Eh? That you'll be seeing your daughter soon? What do your bloody voices say now, Eléonore?"

He stood across from her, his eyes reddened by madness. Paul Vermont, who was usually the picture of composure and elegance, had lost control.

"It's all your fault! It all started the day you told me you were hearing voices! Do you remember? The second summer we spent at Mouettes Beach? Not long after, contracts for the factory were thin on the ground, as were your lucid moments. The employees started to doubt me. And then you left us. You placed the neck I used to kiss in that noose, and you left us for your whispers. Things only got worse at the factory after that. And now . . . Couldn't you be the patron goddess of the dead *and* the living, Eléonore?"

Four hours later, once he had worked up the energy to sit up on the floor where he had collapsed, Paul Vermont saw two yellow beams of light cut through the darkness. The car parked in the drive, a door slammed shut, and the gravel crunched under the visitor's feet. Paul got up and made his way to the gun locker in the cellar. He heard a light knocking at the door. "Come on in, Franck, come in and explain it to me," he mumbled as he loaded a rifle. "Come and explain how you failed to protect my daughter . . ."

He returned to the lounge and hid in a corner, his gun pointed towards the front door, waiting for Red to step inside. After another series of knocks, the doorknob turned, and a hesitant shadow moved towards him.

Paul took aim.

Across from him, his wife's portrait glimmered in the half-light.

He thought he could see her smile.

He thought he could see the waves behind her writhing like snakes.

He thought he could hear a voice telling him to shoot.

But it wasn't Eléonore who had spoken.

It was his daughter.

"Kill him. Make him regret it."

The voice of a broken promise.

"Mr Vermont? It's Franck . . . I came straight here . . ."

Paul let him take a few more steps inside and get close enough to make retreat impossible. Then he came out of his hiding place and pointed his rifle at Red who, looking as pale as a mortal man who had crossed over the rainbow of the dead, immediately raised his hands in the air. "Please don't do that, boss," he begged. "Let me explain. I had no choice."

I

"So?" I asked. We had just left Paul Vermont's house, and it seemed doubtful that we would ever see him again. The man's emaciated body had shaken our hands with all the strength of a child. He had bid us goodbye in a barely audible voice and had slowly, clumsily closed the door. Every minute he had spent answering our questions appeared to have cost him years off his life.

"His testimony wouldn't be admissible in court," Henri noted as he sat down in the passenger seat.

"And he didn't say anything more than he did yesterday," I said regretfully as we got back on the road. "Ghosts, that bloody poem . . ."

"You're forgetting about Auntie."

"That's true. He didn't exactly admit it, but I think we're on the right track."

"All we have to do now is find her. I'm still in touch with my former superior. Maybe I can ask him a few questions. And ask him to look up Mrs Vermont's sister to help us find her mysterious housekeeper . . . I'll also look into the significance of fire and water. Maybe it has to do with some sort of ritual or something."

"Fire and water?"

"Yes, there's a duality there. Fire for Julie and water for Emilie. It struck me at the time. Then Olivier was charged and . . ."

"That's a good idea," I agreed. "Thank you for your help, Henri. I'm sorry I was so distrustful at first."

"You're welcome. I know a mother who will be relieved to learn that her son is innocent."

"And a legal system that will be embarrassed to have been so easily fooled . . . Are you sure you really want to be part of this?"

"I've been waiting for this moment for over thirty years."

I parked my four-by-four next to Henri's Fiat. I offered him a drink before his drive home. He happily accepted ("But no cognac, okay?"). We sat down in the kitchen and drank in silence. I suddenly felt a wave of weariness settle over me, as if carried by the sea breeze which caressed the dunes outside. The recent events also seemed to have left their mark on Henri. Dark circles sat under his eyes reddened by fatigue and this seemingly unsolvable mystery. During the drive, he had developed several different plans for reaching Auntie.

"I can feel that we're close," I said as I polished off my cognac. "But strangely, I'm not sure I want to uncover the truth."

"Whatever we find out, it won't be pretty. But we have to finish this. For Olivier. For Julie. For Emilie. For the innocent souls we were back then."

"What if my mother is guilty?" I asked anxiously.

Henri didn't know what to say. He had already considered the possibility. Back then, but more recently as well. Maybe the disgruntled employees hadn't stopped at threatening letters and arson. "I have a hard time imagining your mother pouring petrol on a child's body and striking a match," he finally said. "We're both exhausted. Let's rest a little before we draw any conclusions that we would later regret. I'm going to go home and sleep for a while, then reach out to my old boss. Let's focus on Auntie for now," he suggested as he stood up.

"You're right. I'm going to clean up this mess. I don't feel like handling Sarah's wrath at the moment!" I joked.

"I'll see you tomorrow morning. Until then, lock all the doors and turn on your alarm."

*

As I stood up to walk Henri to the door and listened to his advice, an idea sparked in my mind.

But then it died just as quickly, like a shooting star.

I frowned and stood still, trying to figure out what had kindled the spark. I repeated the last words I'd heard. It had to have been them. *I'll see you tomorrow morning. Until then, lock all the doors and turn on your alarm.*

The last line of the Malherbe poem popped into my head. *The space of one brief morn.*

It had come to me as though an invisible mouth had whispered it in my ear.

I pushed the strange sensation aside, promising myself that I would analyse it properly once I was alone because Henri, who was walking to his car, had just turned around.

"By the way, what kind of books do you write?" he asked, looking genuinely interested.

"Thrillers," I replied, surprised to meet someone who had never read anything I'd written.

"And how do they end?"

"Badly, most of the time."

"In that case, I'm glad I don't fit the mould of your characters! That means there's a chance this will end well!"

Then he ducked to slide his tall frame into the tiny Fiat. No, he was nothing like the detectives in my novels who fought crime with a combination of whisky, cigarettes, and poor aim. He was just a tired man who had been fighting for thirty years to prove the innocence of a school friend. I felt like I could write a whole book about his struggle. And for the first time since I'd moved there, I wanted to leave my house of steel and glass; I wanted to follow someone else and get *involved*. And I would, once all of this was over. *Yes, I'll take Sarah to the Isle of Yeu and I'll have a nice dinner with Henri. That sounds like a plan!* I said to myself as I went inside.

Just a few seconds later, however, my plans already seemed compromised. After locking the front door, I headed towards the French windows in the lounge. It was there that I found myself staring down the barrel of a rifle.

And holding it, standing tall and determined, was the pirate from my childhood.

"Sit down!" Franck ordered.

I did as I was told, my eyes glued to the gun pointing at me. Red came closer and his scar seemed even more noticeable than in my memories. I focused all my energy on combatting the fear that was rushing through my veins and stopping my hands from trembling as Julie and Emilie's murderer sat down in the armchair across from me. The observation round lasted a few minutes and left me with little hope for the outcome of our confrontation: there was no way out. I would have to fight this man. And more problematic still: I had no weapon and was paralyzed by fear.

"I see yesterday's visit wasn't enough," said Franck regretfully.

"What . . . What do you want?" I managed to reply.

"I just want you to forget, David."

"Why?"

"You know why. Don't play dumb."

"Because you killed Julie and Emilie? Because an innocent man has been stuck in prison for the past thirty years because of you?"

The monster from my childhood listened to these accusations with a small smile on his lips. Never had a smile seemed so revolting.

"I did what I had to do," admitted Franck.

"Kill two girls . . .?"

"Exactly. I understand that's incomprehensible for you,

but there was a reason. And the same reason has brought me here, today, all these years later, to ask you nicely to forget all about it."

"Nicely?" I asked sceptically, gesturing towards the rifle he had trained on me.

"That's just in case you choose the hard way."

"What are you going to do, then? Kill me? You'll have to kill Henri, Samuel and Mr Vermont, too . . . Plus the other people I've told about all this."

"That won't be necessary for Mr Vermont. He doesn't have much time left. As for the 'other people', I think you're bluffing. Given how few visitors you have and how rarely you leave the house, I don't think you're a big fan of nights out with mates, sharing secrets over a few beers . . ."

"Fuck off!"

"Oh, have I touched a nerve? Is that why that pretty brunette left here angry last week? Is that why she had that sad glint in her eye when I spoke to her at the estate agency?"

I immediately understood the implied threat in his words.

"If you touch her, I swear to God, I'll—"

"You're in no position to threaten me. If you stop poking around and let the dead rest in peace, you'll have nothing to worry about."

"What are we about to find out that you're willing to take such risks for?"

"A treasure that should stay at the bottom of the sea," Franck replied enigmatically. "I'll say it again: it would be best for everyone if you let it go. They're dead, and nothing can bring them back. No magic spells. No manuscripts in brown paper envelopes."

"Nothing but memories," I argued, my eyes still on the rifle. "That's why Auntie sent us the text, so I would go back through my repressed memories and turn them back into images, sounds, smells, and whispers . . ."

"Whispers are dangerous, David. They cloud your mind,

slow your heart, and steal your smiles . . . Do you remember how your stepfather used to beat your mother and then take out the rest of his anger on you?"

"Yes, but I also remember Julie and her face, the grain of sand stuck to her skin, her voice and how happy she was when we first saw the fairy lights at the Twisted Wood arcade . . . And I won't let her go again. I'm sorry, but I won't forget."

I didn't know where this courage was coming from. I had decided not to back down, not to hide like I had as a kid when Red had terrified me so much that I would cross the room without looking up. If my stepfather had been sitting across from me, I would have slit his throat. If my mother had been there in Franck's place, I would have berated her for accepting the violence and then taken her in my arms and apologized for not doing it more often when I had the chance. If Julie had been alive, I would have professed my love. If Eléonore hadn't hanged herself, I would have convinced her that the only whispers that matter are those of the living.

In fact, it was more than courage, it was an open revolt against myself and the mistakes I had made. What if *this* was what Auntie had been after when she had sent me the manuscript?

"Are you really stupid enough to believe that I'm not determined to make you change your mind?" asked Red, incredulous.

"I don't think monsters are ever as scary as in our childhood memories. I'm not afraid of you any more. I'm not a little boy any more . . ."

That's the last thing I said . . .

The last thing I said before a deafening blast filled the room.

And instead of my life flashing before my eyes, the first stanza of the poem appeared against my closed eyelids, like the credits on a cinema screen:

But she was of the world, which fairest things exposes . . .

*

When I opened my eyes again, my ears were ringing. The smell of gunpowder wafting through the air implied that the immediate threat was over but I knew that hunting rifles could hold two cartridges . . . Across from me, where there had once been French windows, there was empty space. Pieces of glass were scattered across the floor, shimmering in the sunlight, putting on their final show before the end.

"Bloody hell! You're a madman!" I shouted as I stood up.

"Bullets made for hunting boar. Loud but effective. Stay where you are."

I sat back down and focused my gaze on the thousands of glass shards.

"Do I have your attention now?" asked Franck.

"Yes," I replied simply.

"Good. Now, here's what we're going to do: I'm not going to kill you. In return, you're going to pretend that you never received the manuscript. You're going to convince your friends that it's all a big joke. Then you'll go back to your life, writing your books and making your wife happy, and everyone will be just fine. Got it?"

"Did she know?"

"Who?"

"My mother. Did she know you were going to kill Julie?"

"Don't you understand what I just said?" asked Red, clearly exasperated. He moved slightly closer, the barrel of the rifle still aimed at my face.

I saw a strange glimmer in his eye. It wasn't murderous rage, or madness, or even fear. Though it took me a few minutes to understand (it's rather difficult to think with a gun pointed at you, give it a try if you don't believe me), the solution slowly came together until it was glaringly obvious: he was fighting ghosts of his own. All I had to do was figure out who they were.

"What about my stepfather? Did he help you burn Julie while Fabien drowned Emilie? Which one of you lit the match that burned down Eléonore's house? Eh? If you want me to forget, I'll need answers. Otherwise waves of questions will keep bringing me back to the shores of 1986! How does it feel to break a promise?"

This time, he glued the barrel to my forehead, a look of determination in his eyes. I was close. Maybe even too close because Franck's index finger was trembling dangerously on the trigger.

"You should have let it go, David. I kept my promise . . . Whatever old man Vermont told you, I kept my promise . . ."

So, this is your Achilles heel, I thought as his eyes brimmed with tears. The monster from my childhood was suddenly ridiculously human.

"You promised to protect her!" I shouted as if Franck was upstairs. "You watched us, you followed us to the arcade, and yet you failed to protect her! Bloody hell, Franck, how does it feel to break your promise?! They were only twelve years old, you nasty old bastard. You killed two twelve-year-old girls!"

I was in a trance. I was screaming so loudly that my throat burned. I spewed questions without a second thought for the gun threatening me or even for the answers that might escape from the mouth of my tortured assailant. In fact, in my fit of rage, I had stood up without realizing it. Nothing mattered in that moment.

"Shut up!" shouted Red. "You don't understand!"

"Explain it to me then! Answer my questions! Paul Vermont trusted you, as did Julie. And why Emilie? Were you practising? Did you promise them everything would be okay before you murdered them?"

"Shut up, I said!"

"How does it feel to break your promise, Franck?"

I had him. I didn't know why (I would find out later, once the full horror of the story was revealed), but Red was losing his confidence and seemed to want to flee rather than listen to my questions. I realized he no longer intended to kill me. Maybe he had never really wanted to. So I repeated the question one last time, a question that appeared to destroy him, certain that those words held more truth than the twelve chapters combined.

"How does it feel to break your promise, Franck?"

"It's killing me," confessed Red, lowering his gun. "That's why he's dead. And that's why I killed them."

3

He?

Had I heard right?

He?

None of the chapters had mentioned a missing boy. My blood turned to ice in seconds at the idea that another child may have been subjected to this man's violent madness. How had this third victim eluded Auntie's story?

Franck sat down in the armchair, still holding the rifle in both hands, though he seemed wholly unaware of it. He didn't even seem to realize that I was there any more. He seemed to be hypnotized by the memory of a house with dark shutters.

"You're right," he sighed finally. "Maybe it is time to end this . . ." He kept his gaze focused on the floor.

I didn't know if he was speaking to me or to the whispers in the memories that tormented him. I didn't dare say a word.

"You just won't let it go, eh?" he asked, looking at me this time.

"No. It's too late now."

"Do you understand your final chapter, David?" he asked in a weary voice.

"No, not yet."

"Well then I have a little time left," said Franck, who now seemed as tired and fragile as Mr Vermont.

I could have tried to seize the gun. Maybe I would have succeeded. Yet a voice in my head told me to wait, to listen to this ghost, because that's what the monster from my childhood was now—a ghost about to disappear.

"Tell me what happens in the other final chapters," he urged.

"Why should I?" I asked.

"Because then I'll tell you why I always keep my promises. And you'll understand who 'he' is."

I don't know why, but I agreed. I took a deep breath and told him the whole story. I wasn't especially keen for the man sitting opposite me to share the details of his most terrible crimes, but I told him everything I could remember. He chuckled when he learned that Samuel had seen him that night, and seemed to regret how quickly the case had been closed. The words poured out of me, freeing me at last from this story and its characters. When I had finished, I noticed that the gun was no longer pointed at me. It was lying on the floor forgotten.

"Did you love her?" he suddenly asked me.

"Yes."

"She loved you, too."

"How do you know?"

"She told me. When we were in that car park. She told me she didn't want to die because she'd never see you again."

"You're a monster . . ."

"I don't deny it," Red replied calmly. "Now let me tell you how I became one. And why I hear a little boy ask me to hold his hand every day. It's your turn to listen to *my* 'final chapter'."

The Final Chapter

The Man with the Scar

I was about the same age as you were that summer when someone I loved more than anything in the world became a ghost.

We lived in a flat near the factory. Every morning my brother and I would watch my father put on his overalls and tousle our hair before heading off to Vermont Steelworks. He was a quiet man who drank and often used his belt to discipline us. But every time he did, we deserved it. At least that's what I told myself as a kid. A few bruises on our bums were nothing next to the joy we felt when he ran his hands through our hair.

It was summer.

School holidays.

I took care of my brother Jérôme every day because my mum worked too and couldn't get any time off that summer. Every morning, before she left, she would make our lunch and leave a five-franc coin on the table. That tiny coin heralded the best moment of the day: when the ice cream van would park in front of our building. If my story stopped here, I'd say I had a pretty happy childhood. Jérôme and I would spend our days playing outside, mostly kicking a ball around. The neighbours kept an eye on us from afar. That day my father told me to look out for my little brother, as he did every day. He made me promise. Every single day. It wasn't psychological torture, just the best way he had found to be able to go to work without worrying during his entire shift. He needed that reassurance more than he needed me to obey, and after a while, the phrase, "Promise you'll look after Jérôme?" became a verbal reflex rather than a real request.

My brother was four years old. When we would hear the ice cream van jingle outside it was Pavlovian; the sound would instantly fill us with joy and we would abandon whatever we were doing to grab the coin from the table and run down the three flights of stairs as if the building were on fire. Once outside, we would walk up the alley and wait on the pavement to cross the road and join the queue of customers, many of whom had got there before the music had even started. Every day, my four-year-old little brother held out his hand before crossing the road and clung to me, eager to be holding a cone of strawberry sorbet in his other hand. I'll never know why. Maybe because he'd spilled a glass of milk on the table two hours earlier. Or because his bedroom, which I had tidied before our parents got home the day before, had looked like a bomb had gone off and he had refused to help me clean it up. Maybe because a promise too often repeated loses its meaning over time . . .

"Can you hold my hand to cross the street, Franck? Will you hold my hand?"

"No, Jérôme, you're big enough to cross on your own now."

"Let's race then!"

Hypnotized by the ice cream van and its sweet delights, neither of us heard the car. The scene only lasted a few seconds, but every time it resurfaces in my mind, I see it in slow motion. Even then, I never have enough time to do anything to protect him. Jérôme took my refusal to hold his hand as an invitation to cross over the road and wait for me on the pavement opposite, where the ice cream vendor was already setting up his van. But he never reached the other side. The car slammed into him and his skull thudded against the radiator grill. I still have a very clear picture of my brother falling heavily onto the tarmac. And the sound. But the car didn't brake. It pulled his lifeless body along far enough for witnesses to run after it shouting at the driver to stop. Jérôme lay there hooked to the undercarriage for a few seconds until the car jumped forward again, freeing him. It ran over his legs, leaving behind the body of the boy I had promised to protect.

I didn't come to my senses until a neighbour grabbed me by the shoulders and shook me. All I remember is telling myself I would lie down next to my brother and take his place so he could go and enjoy his ice cream. But when I tried to get closer, adults blocked my path. An elderly neighbour took me in her arms as she wept. I wanted to tell her there was no need to be so upset, that everything was okay, that Jérôme was just pretending to be asleep, like when our parents tucked us in at night. But another neighbour was crying, too. A man. He was kneeling over my brother and his hands were covered in blood. That's when I realized what had happened.

I started crying, too.

The rest is hard to remember. The ambulance. My parents arriving at the hospital. The doctor as white as his coat. My seemingly endless solitude. My open hand waiting desperately to hold a smaller one. The drive home in silence. And time ticking past—never fast enough for me to forget.

"You promised to protect him," my father said a week after my brother's funeral.

As I had watched the tiny coffin being lowered into the ground, I was convinced that there had been a mistake. There was no way that that insignificant box could hold Jérôme. He was much more than that, so much more.

"I didn't see the car . . . It all happened so fast . . ."

"You promised," mumbled my father.

"I miss him, Dad," I cried, hoping he would comfort me.

My father had been a drinker even before the accident. Now, he drank even more. Beer bottles were piled up around him. He took hold of one and emptied it out. Then he grabbed it by the neck and broke it against the edge of the table.

"Come here," he ordered.

"You cut yourself, Dad. Your hand's bleeding," I said as I went to him.

"Your mother will fix me up when she gets home. Come here."

As I said earlier, children convince themselves that their punishments are deserved. They do it for themselves, so it will be over more quickly. So they can get back to what they would usually be doing that day. But they also do it for the people they love, the people they've upset. Their fiercest desire at that moment is not to escape the punishment, but for it to be over and done with so that life can get back to normal. The pain is a detail. Think of something else. Think of your morning routine. Mum's smile. The hot chocolate she lovingly prepares. Your father's hand in your hair. His face, which will someday be yours. The sense that you are a source of constant joy in their lives . . .

"I'm sorry," I pleaded, moving closer so that he would take me in his arms. "I miss him so much . . ."

"You made me a promise," my father whispered in my ear as he massaged my scalp hard and clumsily with his free hand instead of stroking me as he usually did.

"I know, I'm sor—"

His hand closed around my hair and pulled my face to his chest. With the other hand he raised the broken bottle to my cheek.

"Promises must always be kept," he said solemnly. "This time I'll make sure you remember that."

The sharp glass cut into my skin with a mixture of sadness and anger.

The child that I was but would never be again understood then that I deserved that punishment more than I had any other.

I couldn't help but stare at his scar. A full ten centimetres long, it stretched down the length of his right cheek. Despite his short beard and the passage of time, it was still Franck's most prominent feature.

His words whirled around inside my head before vanishing. If he hadn't killed two girls, I would probably have been more affected by his distress and his memories. Though the image of a little boy being brutally run over like that was horrifying, the thought of Red leaning over Julie and Emilie, a murderous smile distorting his scar, erased any compassion I might have felt for him.

We were suddenly met with a cool breeze, which blew in through the shattered French windows, bringing with it the smell of the sea. It was getting late and the darkness would soon be as enigmatic and impenetrable as the man sitting across from me.

So that's what your ghosts are whispering, Franck, I thought, looking down. *You are haunted not only by Jérôme (*Can you hold my hand to cross the street?*), but also by Emilie and Julie (*Will I become a ghost?*) and your father (*You made me a promise . . .*).*

Far too many first deaths to avoid the descent into madness . . .

"Why did you tell me all that?" I finally asked.

"To help you," replied Franck resignedly.

"To help me?"

"To help you understand. Believe me, once you figure out your final chapter, you'll have all the answers to your questions. It's a beautiful poem. Did you know that Eléonore named her dog Malherbe after the poet?"

I hadn't known and didn't really care to be honest.

"If you really want to help me," I said, "tell me where to find Auntie."

"Auntie . . . I'm sorry, but I don't think that's a good idea."

"You're going to run, aren't you?"

"Yes, I'm going to disappear. You're close to the truth. And as you have guessed, once you tell them what you know, the police will want to ask me a few questions . . . I don't have a choice, really. Or rather, the other choice would be to kill you and the others—not only those who received the manuscripts, but also Auntie, Mr Vermont, Olivier . . . But I can't even shoot you. There's still too much of the boy I knew in you . . . And you still need to decipher your last chapter."

"I don't give a shit about my last chapter. I understand the big picture: Auntie sent us the texts to prove one man's innocence and inculpate another. I couldn't care less about your promises—broken or not—just like I couldn't care less about Malherbe. The only thing that matters now is that you pay for what you've done . . ."

"I pay for it every day, believe me."

"Why did you kill Emilie?"

"A . . . A practice run, like you said earlier. I had to know if I could really do it."

"You're crazy . . ."

"David," sighed Red as he picked up the rifle.

"You're a murderer. A madman."

"Am I? And what about your parents? Your mother? Wasn't she crazy to accept your stepfather's violence? Do you think she knew nothing about our plans? She was there at every meeting! She watched the house burn down without saying a word, too! Do you really think I'm the only murderer in this story? The murderer isn't necessarily the only one responsible for death. There are also those who encourage him. With their presence. Their silence. They were all murderers. Julie stood no chance!"

"And yet you're the one who took their lives! You killed two girls just like you killed your brother!"

I was perfectly lucid. I knew that when he heard that final accusation, he would pick up the rifle and shoot me. That's how I would die. The next day, Sarah would come home to find a ransacked lounge, shattered French windows, and her husband's face blown to pieces, a gruesome mixture of bone, blood, and brains. The gulls would undoubtedly pick their way through the chaos to scavenge what they could.

I would have liked to have more time.

That's what people think before they die.

I would have liked to have more time.

A little more time to find Auntie.

A little more time to figure out the truth.

A little more time to finally say hello to the old woman with the dog who walks along the beach each morning.

A little more time to get to know Henri.

A little more time to take Sarah to the Isle of Yeu.

But the gun never fired. Instead, there were a few final words. And the feeling that nothing made sense.

"You're still just a kid, David. You'll finally understand when you figure out what your last chapter really means. I suppose this is goodbye."

I sat there, perfectly still in my chair, for a long time.

An hour.

Maybe several.

A heavy, repulsive silence invaded the house. The sound of the waves in the distance struggled to provide a steady rhythm for the cacophony inside my head. I couldn't think amid all the noise—so many words. All the final chapters seemed to blend together, creating a concert of voices: Julie, Emilie, Jérôme, my stepfather, my mother. And they were joined in their macabre dance by the lines from Malherbe's poem. Each of the characters and all of the memories were conveying a message, but I still couldn't translate it.

After a long while, I came back to life and got out of the armchair I sat in every morning to watch the horizon as I waited for inspiration to strike. I would have to stop that habit now . . . I didn't know what to do. Should I phone Henri to tell him about my discussion with Red? Let him call the police? Forget about it all and make up excuses to explain to Sarah why the house and I were in such a state? Tell Samuel that he had been right, that everyone around us had become a ghost?

The only decision I was able to make was to pick up the bookcases and books and put them back in their place, restoring a sliver of normality.

I tried to forget.

For the first time since the envelope had appeared on my porch, I focused not on finding the answers to the mystery, but on pushing each of the escaped ghosts back down into the forgotten depths. I was a wave trying not to caress the shore but to flee it, fighting against the current of my thirst for knowledge.

Was Red right? Was it best to forget about it? To erase the memories? Wouldn't the ghosts just keep coming back, as stubborn as the tides? Wouldn't the spectral voices of Eléonore, Julie and Emilie keep singing me morbid songs that would send me to my death, in the same way that they had tormented Mr Vermont?

As I knelt down to pick up my books, I felt the spark of a new idea. I fought its presence for a few seconds, but it kept coming back, getting louder and brighter every time I looked closer at it. I tried in vain to escape its reach, but the spark soon grew into a raging fire around which the voices gathered, clearer than ever before, like pirate souls around a sacred pyre. My body swayed like a ship lost at sea and I had to sit down on the floor to keep from toppling over.

★

The voices grew louder still. They crossed the ocean, time, my childhood, and Avenue des Mouettes to gather like pieces of a jigsaw puzzle. Pieces of the dead fit together with pieces of the living, as if there were no real barrier between them.

A promise is a promise.
> *But she was of the world, which fairest things exposes*

Will I become a ghost?
> *To fates the most forlorn;*

Listen to the whispers.
> *A rose, she too hath lived as long as live the roses,*

This is all really one big ghost story.
> *The space of one brief morn.*

Whatever old man Vermont told you, I kept my promise . . .

And suddenly it all made sense.

The truth hit me.

And it was as shocking and senseless as a woman hanging herself to join the whispers from the sea. "And yet, Eléonore was right," I admitted to myself vaguely, terrified by my revelation.

That's where I would find the other end of the rainbow.

And that's where I was headed in the morning.

The next morning, after a restless night spent convincing myself that I was losing my mind, I made my way down the shingle path to the beach at eight o'clock sharp.

Golden rays of sunshine reflected off the surface of the ocean. The water was calm and lethargic. Birds pecking nervously at the sand along the shoreline were untroubled by the hesitant little waves.

I sat down a few metres from the water with a steaming cup of coffee in my hand. Despite myself, I checked that not a single drop had stained the porcelain rim. There were dark tears near the bottom of the cup. Not from the unlevel ground, but from my trembling hands.

I put the cup down next to me and wrapped my arms around my knees, clutching them to my chest. I stared at the sea for several minutes. As though it might contain the truth. As though Emilie's body might finally emerge. As though pirates in rags might appear from the waves and walk towards the shore to convince me that I was wrong, that being here at this time of day was as hopeless and ridiculous as their belief in a patron goddess.

But the ocean remained quiet.

It refused to reveal any secrets, refused to confirm or refute my theory.

So I waited.

And tried to convince myself yet again that it was impossible.

I waited quite some time before I noticed movement in the distance. I immediately recognized him. The golden retriever was knee-deep in the surf when he caught sight of me and froze. He studied me for a few seconds, then trotted over, his head held high, ignoring the angry squawks of the seabirds in his path. He lay down next to me, his jet-black eyes contemplating the tears streaming down my cheeks.

I stroked him awkwardly, unable to wrench my gaze from the horizon. The dog seemed unbothered, happy to enjoy the affection as he too looked in the direction from which he'd come.

Certain memories refuse to disappear completely. Our first deaths among them. And the colourful fairy lights at the Twisted Wood arcade. Monsters and mothers. Hanged women and poets. Drowning girls. Burning girls. Boys crushed like forgotten promises. They all come together to create the rainbow that the pirates from our childhood cross from time to time, invited by a scent, a flavour, a vision, or a manuscript found on a doorstep. They are the whispers we have to learn to live with.

That's what I had come to understand during the night.

And sometimes, those memories could become as real and tangible as a sentence spoken not far away.

A sentence that transformed my tears into sobs.

And kept me glued to the sand.

And woke the dog dozing at my side.

"There you are, Donkey! Leave the man . . ."

The new arrival sat down beside us.

Her feet entered my field of vision but stayed at a safe distance, as if an invisible wall were there to keep us from sharing a grain of sand as we once had.

I still couldn't move. Even though I had uncovered the truth that night when I had finally deciphered my final chapter, part of me was still certain that it was pure madness. But there was no room left for doubt now. The meaning of Mr Vermont's words, "This is all really one big ghost story", was finally clear.

"I see you figured out your final chapter," said Julie in a voice so real it made me shiver.

"You . . . You're dead."

"Yes, David, I died further down this same beach in the summer of 1986."

"I feel like I'm losing my mind," I said, my gaze focused on the sand between my feet.

"Luckily you were still smart enough to suss out the poem," Julie tried to joke. "I knew you'd get there. I've read all your books, you know. I'm a huge fan!"

"Why? Why didn't you explain when we were kids?" I asked, ignoring her digression and drying my tears with the back of my hand.

"Why didn't you kiss me that night?"

"Because I didn't understand . . . Because I was scared."

"Well then you know why I didn't say anything," she replied. "I was a child. I was frightened. My parents' house was burning down. The sky was filled with smoke. Franck turned up and told me we had to leave quickly, that I was in danger. We went to get the car from the car park, where Samuel saw us. I saw him, too. I tried to get his attention, but I don't think he noticed. I got into the back, all my stuff was already there. We drove all night. I didn't ask any questions, since that was what we had agreed with my father when he decided to let me visit Mouettes Beach. My trust in my father was absolute. And he trusted Franck just as much. We stopped once. He made a phone call, and when he came back, I could see he was crying. So, I got comfortable in the back seat and pretended to be asleep, hoping that the year would go by as quickly as possible so that I could see you again."

I tried to muster enough courage to look up from the sand and into Julie's eyes. I didn't manage it.

"So, the body . . ."

"I only found out years later. I grew up in England, in a tiny village in Suffolk. My aunt and I got on a flight the day after I returned from Saint-Hilaire. I didn't understand what was happening. Everyone around me said not to ask questions.

They said someday I'd understand, but for now I had to do as I was told. Later, when I was a teenager and my father came to see me, I tried to get answers, but my questions overwhelmed him with sadness, so I made do with his vague replies. 'Mouettes Beach is cursed, sweetheart. And it's partly my fault. Forget about that summer.' That was the only explanation that ever crossed his lips. The years went by and I forgot."

I couldn't hold it against her. Avenue des Mouettes had disappeared from my own memories for quite a few years.

"Then my father fell ill," she continued. "I came back to France three months ago to take care of him. Julie Malherbe, formerly Julie Vermont, took up residence in a hotel in Saint-Jean-de-Monts. I walked along the beach and past your house, without thinking for a second that I would soon be stepping through your gate and placing a brown envelope containing a terrible secret on your doorstep. But one afternoon, while I was out shopping, I heard on the local radio that a man convicted of two murders was about to be set free. They cited the names of the victims: Julie and Emilie. And a date: 1986. I went straight back to my father's house, because something told me it couldn't be a coincidence. That's when he explained it all, including the body."

"Emilie . . ."

"Emilie," whispered Julie. "I learned that Franck had decided to kill a young girl to fake my death. I was so angry that I couldn't believe my ears. I even slapped my dying father. Red had told my father that on that Friday, the night you arrived, he had attended a meeting at your bungalow. He had left drunk and furious. After a long walk along the beach to try to calm down, he had come across a young girl at the edge of the wood, near the Twisted Wood arcade. She looked so much like me that he had called out to her using my name. Emilie had been crying because she couldn't find her way back to the camp site. He had gone to her, whispering my name and that of a little boy. Emilie had trusted him. She had held his hand and listened as he promised to take her back to her parents. She had been shivering from the cold, so he had taken her in his arms. He had held her close. Too close. He had been confused when she went quiet. *Julie . . . Jérôme . . . I miss him, too, Dad . . . A promise is a promise . . . I miss him so much . . .* Emilie was suffocated by a man who wanted to strangle the past. When Franck realized that he had just murdered a child, he got scared. He picked up the body before anyone could spot them and ran back to the beach with Emilie in his arms. He wanted to throw her in, hand her over to the currents. He wanted the pirates to watch over her and wash away the madness and the crimes—the one his colleagues were preparing and the one he'd just committed . . . *Standing there across from the very same ocean we would watch together a few days later on our way back from the arcade,* was undoubtedly the moment when Red realized that there might be a solution. *God, I'm alive because she died . . . How could I live with that? I had to bring the truth to light. David, my father is the one who told me where you lived. He's the one who came up with the idea to send you a text.*"

"Bloody hell, he killed her to protect you. He kept his promise," I said with a sigh, thinking back to Franck's last words.

I slowly raised my head and looked out over the water. Emilie's body hadn't been thrown into the sea after all. Red had hidden it and then burned it to fake Julie's death. Samuel had been right when he had said that the missing girl looked just like Julie. That detail had undoubtedly helped Franck to hatch his plan. Since there was no DNA evidence at the time, once her body was charred, the legal system, in its rush to close the case, had simply followed the clues left by the murderer.

"So your father told you the truth and wanted you to write it for me?"

"Yes. I think he had been waiting to be free of this secret since the night I left Saint-Hilaire and Franck confessed what he had done. My father almost killed him you know. He waited for him with a loaded rifle. I was still pretending to be asleep when Franck went inside. Ten minutes later, my father came running out, opened the car door, and took me in his arms, crying tears I didn't understand. From that moment on, the two men were bound by a secret that, if it got out, would send them both to prison for the rest of their lives. My father promised Franck that he would never talk as long as he disappeared for good. And the next day I left for England."

"What about Auntie?" I asked, thinking back to the woman who had been at the heart of the story since the beginning.

"She died a year after they found the body . . . She killed herself. An overdose. I only found out when I returned to France," Julie explained, her voice trailing off sadly.

Learning that Auntie had taken her own life made me clench my fists in anger. I saw her silhouette again, following Julie like a guardian angel. I remembered our first meeting—"You must be David!"—and the smiles we exchanged. But more than anything, I remembered how happy and safe I felt in her presence. She was an adult. Just like my stepfather and Red. Just like my mother and her vacant eyes. And Samuel's brother. But she wasn't dangerous. She was an adult who could still hear the voices from her own childhood.

"I'm sorry," I mumbled. "I really liked her."

"I know," was all Julie said.

"You know what all of this means?" I asked suddenly, looking up towards the sky.

"What?"

"Red murdering Emilie," I specified, cursing the conclusion I had come to.

"That he's crazy?" said Julie.

"No, it's not as simple as that unfortunately. It means that he thought you were in enough danger to act recklessly to protect you. As you said, he was drunk and angry, but he must have been scared too, frightened by the determination of the people he'd just left behind at the bungalow. Which means that my stepfather and his friends really did intend to kill you."

"None of that matters," Julie interrupted.

"It does to me."

"I'm sure your mother—"

"Red wasn't so sure. He did say that my mother never would have been able to hurt you. I guess he wanted to protect me, or at least my memories of her. But he also said that the murderer isn't necessarily the only one responsible for death. There are also those who encourage him. And I think he's right . . ."

"Maybe he's just crazy and made it all up . . ." Julie suggested generously.

I closed my eyes for a moment and saw a little boy holding out his hand for someone to take it to cross the street. I was lost. All this information—not to mention the sudden reappearance of my childhood love who hadn't just vanished but had been dead for thirty years—was too much for my brain. A single question emerged, and I was sure she had wondered the same thing: should we condemn Red for killing Emilie or thank him for saving Julie?

I refused to answer. My indecision left a nauseating taste in my mouth.

"When did you figure out your final chapter?" asked Julie, who was beginning to feel uncomfortable with the silence.

"Last night, thanks to Franck."

"He came to see you?"

"Twice. My French windows may never recover. He told me that your mother's dog was called Malherbe. That's what put me on the right track. That and the last line of the poem: *The space of one brief morn.* It seemed these two clues were pointing me towards the old woman I had seen walking past my house every morning with her golden retriever. I was sure that it was Auntie. Then, and I'm still not sure why, I went back to the first line of the poem: *But she was of the world, which fairest things exposes.* The use of the singular bothered me. The poem is about one girl whereas the manuscript was about two bodies. Either it was just an oversight and the author got lazy when choosing the poem (which didn't seem likely given all of the specific details in the manuscript), or it was a clue. And that's when your father's words came back to me like an echo. 'This is all really one big ghost story. About the dead who come back to life . . . And about the living who are already dead . . . They're all ghosts. And they all have a message to share . . . If you really want to know the truth, you'll have to learn to believe in ghosts. There's no other way.' I fought the idea all night. It seemed unbelievable and made me feel like I was losing my mind. To get rid of that feeling, there was only one thing left to do.

"Meet the 'old woman'."

"I'm sorry, but from a distance . . ."

"Yes, distance and time make things harder to see . . . And it's true that I have a slight limp at the moment. A recent fracture. It's my fault Franck is here. I sent him a letter to let him know that my father didn't have much time left. I hesitated for ages, but I decided he deserved to know. I knew my father had gone to see him and had probably warned him that the truth would come out."

"But you weren't even in France then. So . . ."

"My father wanted to go to the police and confess. He'd planned to do it just before Olivier got out of prison. Then he was diagnosed, and I came to be with him. He told me everything and guessed that the best way to get a writer to believe the truth was to dress it up as fiction. Pretty twisted. But I argued that sending it to only one person was risky. If you didn't react, we would have lost precious time. So I decided to draft three versions, each with its own final chapter."

"Why didn't you just come to see me and tell me all this?"

"What would I have said?" she retorted defensively as she picked up a handful of sand. 'Hi, it's me, I've been dead for thirty years but I think I know who really did it?' You were the three people with the most reason to want to understand what really happened. I had to take you back to the past, remind you who you were back then and why each of you should have listened, should have spoken out, and should have looked; the deaf man, the silent man and the blind man. Our memories are ravaged by time, but I was convinced that memories from three different people would eventually lead to the truth."

"Why am I the main character?" I asked.

"Because you always have been for me. And because your role isn't over yet."

"It's not?"

"No, David. You have something very important to do. Now it's your turn to make a promise."

I listened to Julie's request.

Donkey was in a deep sleep, soothed by the sound of our voices and the rhythmic waves.

I still hadn't worked up the courage to look Julie in the face. In fact, it seemed like she was avoiding looking directly at me, too, as though we'd both decided to speak to the children we had once been rather than to the adults we were now. Out of the corner of my eye, I could vaguely make out her hair, which seemed less blonde than in my memories. Would her face be the same if I dared look? Would the young Julie's grin disappear from my memory forever if I caught sight of this woman's smile? It was a risk I refused to take. Dead or alive, Julie could never be as beautiful as she was in my memories. Of that I was sure.

"So, you want me to write a book?" I asked.

"Yes."

"But the courts will correct their mistake," I replied.

"That's why you'll publish it in six months' time, when Olivier gets out of prison. My father won't live much longer. He won't have to brave the media firestorm."

"What about you?"

"I'll be far away, David. I'm only visiting."

"Why do you want—"

"For Emilie," she said, cutting me off. "For her parents . . . For Auntie. For Olivier who never hurt a soul . . . For the children we were, who promised to never grow old. For our first kiss stolen by the waves, for Henri and his fight for the truth, for my mother and her ghosts . . . There are so many reasons. You can unveil the truth using the chapters I gave you.

There are enough details there for you to turn them into a real novel."

"And then?"

"And then the book will be published, and you can pretend it's a work of pure fiction. But a former police officer will take things further. Henri will do his best to convince his old colleagues that it could be true."

"Why not just send the text to the police?"

"Because I want people to remember, David. I want Emilie's name to be on everyone's lips, I want them all to know that she died so I could live. I want the pirates to free her so that she can come and sit here next to us. And the only way a ghost can cross the rainbow is when people tell her story, read it, and say her name aloud. Because when the whispers stop, all that's left is silence and sadness, David."

Julie was right. The best way to seek justice was to get as many people as possible to speak Emilie's name. Then no one would be able to ignore it any longer, including the judges, the press, and the police. I would be the one to help her cross the rainbow. That was the promise I made to Julie.

I lost myself for a moment in the slow, gentle movement of the rising tide as it swallowed the beach. Waves have always reminded me of hands trying in vain to hold onto the present as they're dragged back to the past.

"It's time to close your gate," suggested Julie as she stood up. "Not only the gate to your property, but also the one that let in all the ghosts. I'm going to close mine, too. You'll receive a letter soon, to give to Henri. Tell him to open it the day Olivier gets out of prison."

"So, this is it? You're just going to disappear again?"

"I'll drop you a line from time to time."

"That's really not very nice," I replied with a smile.

Alerted by his owner's movements, Donkey stood up and leaned in for one last stroke.

"Tell Samuel I said hello. And tell him Donkey would have liked to meet him."

"I'm sure he'll appreciate the reference," I said as I stood up in turn.

Just then, in a fit of bravery, I looked into Julie's eyes. They were still emerald-green and though they were more tired than they had once been, they were still bright. Her hair was shorter and her smile, which had once kindled unspeakable desire in me, was more reserved. We stayed there for a moment, face to face, reproducing the scene in which the kiss had never happened, where two children had believed in the immortality of a friendship bracelet, voicing without realizing it the same hope that they would never forget each other.

Then Julie turned and began her long walk back to her father, the man who had begun this story and who would end it. The man I had assumed was crazy when he told me to believe in the ghosts of the past.

Epilogue
(added for the second edition)

Six months later

Sarah is by my side.

Henri too.

Full of emotion, the three of us watch as a man approaches the front gate of Roche-sur-Yon prison.

Twenty other people are present.

It takes Olivier a little while to realize that they are all here for him. Henri pushes Olivier's mother in her wheelchair. Her eyes are brimming with tears. She mumbles painful excuses when her son leans in and takes her in his arms. The small crowd gathers around the man who—though he doesn't know it yet, since Samuel has scheduled publication for the next day—will soon attract the attention of the entire country. Of course, I couldn't resist the temptation to let his mother read it ahead of time, and she shared it with the rest of the family. The process was underway. The old woman had begun to speak Olivier's name again, and then so had the neighbours. They had all promised to be present on the day he left prison. I also see a journalist. He must be wondering who sent him a brown envelope containing a few excerpts from the book. Maybe he'll investigate and find his way to me. For the moment, he's taking pictures.

All in good time.

Henri goes over to Olivier. They hug and I can see tears in the former police officer's eyes. I swallow my own and Sarah kisses my cheek.

An hour later, when Olivier, his mother, Sarah, Henri, a solicitor I hired, and I sit down in the private room of a Michelin-starred restaurant, an envelope appears.

"This is for you, Olivier," Henri announces as he slides it towards his friend. "I don't know what's inside. I was just told to give it to you."

I watch knowingly as Olivier opens it. He pulls out a piece of paper bearing just two words—*I'm sorry*—followed by a line of numbers and letters as well as an address. A few days later, Olivier learns that he has an account in his name at the local bank in Saint-Hilaire-de-Riez that has been receiving secret deposits for years. The only information he can access is the amount available in the account: three hundred and ten thousand euros. Ten thousand euros for each year he spent in prison.

Henri and I tell Olivier about the book and how it came to be. He listens carefully but doesn't seem to really understand what it all means. He'll need some time. After thirty-one years fighting the system, he's a sceptical man.

Paul Vermont joined Eléonore three months after the book came out. He was buried in the cemetery located just a few metres from the ruins of the old factory, next to the graves of his wife and Julie. The remains in Julie's coffin were exhumed by forensics teams once the case was reopened and the request for DNA evidence was approved.

A warrant was immediately issued for Franck's arrest. The police found him quickly, at his home. He'd hanged himself. When they questioned her, Nana Côte d'Or informed them that the porch light had been out for several weeks.

As a result of the judges' most recent decisions, an official ceremony will be held in which the French government will officially recognize Olivier's innocence.

Every now and again, I get a blank postcard without a single word or return address. They all feature seascapes. In each of them, the blue water contrasts with the orange sun in the sky above.

There's no tone-on-tone that blurs the border between the two, like in the photograph in my bedroom, and no rainbow filtering the living and the dead.

In the images Julie sends me, everything is crystal clear. Tranquil. Peaceful.

Like our childhood should have been.

Like a perfect first kiss.

Acknowledgments

First and foremost, I would like to express my heartfelt thanks and gratitude to Caroline Lépée and Philippe Robinet. Without you, this story would have been nothing more than a whisper.

Thank you to the whole team at Calmann-Lévy. I won't name names because I'm afraid I might forget someone, and you all deserve recognition. Your advice, corrections, and kindness have made me feel supported and encouraged since the beginning. You are the precious crew without which no ship would ever set sail.

Thank you also to the police officer Julien B. for his invaluable help and advice (and I apologize for kicking you during football practice!).

Thank you to Julie F. for "lending" me her name. You see, *a promise is a promise* . . .

Some of the places/characters/events mentioned really do exist. The advantage of fiction is that the author may embellish or darken them as he pleases.

So I made the most of it.

So, thank you to the redhead from my childhood, who may have been a secret agent, an assassin, a pirate, or just a normal guy.

Thank you to my mother for taking me to Mouettes Beach. Given that the statute of limitations has expired, I can now admit that one night when I slept over at a friend's house, we really did sneak out to the Twisted Wood (*Le Bois Tordu*) arcade.

Thank you to the little boy who got run over on the Rue Sarrault and luckily survived. I always wanted to thank you for fighting so hard. Now I have, thanks to you.

Thank you to Sophie H., my first reader and the light of my son's life.

Thank you to Loan, who, as I write these lines, is singing "Get Out of Your Own Way" without taking any notice of the actual lyrics or my presence.

I'm fighting the urge to join in, but it's a losing battle.

Get out of my own way . . .

I'm in a hurry to get this over with so I can sing too.

That's the way it is and I'm not complaining.

The fight is over.

Childhood wins.